# TICKLED KINK

First Edition

Published by The Nazca Plains Corporation
Las Vegas, Nevada
2007

ISBN: 978-1-934625-49-1

Published by

The Nazca Plains Corporation ®
4640 Paradise Rd, Suite 141
Las Vegas NV 89109-8000

PUBLISHER'S NOTE
*Tickled Kink* is a work of fiction created wholly by the imagination of the authors named herein. All characters are fictional and any resemblance to any persons living or deceased is purely by accident. No portion of this book reflects any real person or events.

Cover, Maxfx
Art Director, Blake Stephens

# DEDICATION

To Ray and Fred, thanks for the smiles

# TICKLED KINK

First Edition

Compiled by Christopher Trevor

# CONTENTS

# INTRODUCTION

## Introduction by constant tickle hero and tickle victim: Timmy Backman

Yes, I do believe the two words "tickle" and "kink" go hand in hand or foot in hand if you would. Maybe as children and adolescents, tickling is just fun and games. But, somewhere during puberty and when the sexual juices begin to flow, tickling switches into the realm of sexual stimulation and "kink." For me, tickling has been a turn on for as long as I've had an "on" switch. And my fantasies have mostly left me as the ticklee as opposed to the tickler. Meeting Christopher Trevor and being fully immersed into the genre of male on male tickling, has taken this straight dude, Timmy Backman, to new heights of tickle sex. Now, not only do I enjoy the aspects of being tickled and dominated by sexy women but, I have the added and expanded stimulation of being tricked, subdued, tickled, sexually stimulated and totally humiliated by dominant male ticklers, hence where the "kink" aspect of all this comes in. Christopher Trevor has opened a whole new vista for me and doomed the straight but ever ticklish and gullible Timmy Backman to suffer at the hands and instruments of the studs who wish to conquer him...and Timmy is such a succulent target. Lets not any of us forget how I wound up kidnapped and tickle tortured by my good buddy Ronald in the soon to be classic tickle novel "Timmy's Ticklish Trials." Oh my word!

# MY SADISTIC TICKLING NEIGHBOR HAL

## Written by: Matt

I have lived in an upscale neighborhood on the outskirts of Dallas for about a year - a transplant from Hurricane Katrina; my wife and I found a nice town and good jobs to help rebuild our lives. One late August afternoon I was in my upstairs bedroom folding some clothes when I heard a raucous laughter coming from our next door neighbor's house. I peered out the window and noticed my neighbor Hal holding his pretty wife's feet in a headlock as they sat by the pool and he seemed to be giving her a nice foot tickling while she laughed and yelled at him to stop. She was obviously ticklish, but in the same breath, not really enjoying it. After a few minutes he released her feet, and she got up very angry and stormed into the house. I found myself very aroused by the whole scene since I have been a closet lover of tickling for years... I noticed Hal stroking himself through his trunks as he sat by the pool and wondered if he too shared my love of tickling. The following weekend we were supposed to join a couple of other neighbors for a cookout at Hal's and thought it would be a dream come true if I could get Hal to somehow tickle my wife like that... Even for a few minutes. I fantasized as I stroked myself and let my mind play out several scenarios. My wife though is not into tickling and several times I have gone over the limit with tickling her and she has gotten very angry with me...so I know any tickling would be by luck...but I promised myself to somehow bring up the subject with Hal next weekend.

All week long I figured I could get the conversation steered toward tickling by just bringing up the episode I witnessed last weekend with Hal. Hal is forty-six years old, six feet one, and two hundred pounds and solidly built with just a hint of gray in his hair. I have seen him working out most days in his home gym. I'm thirty-eight years old, six feet tall, one hundred and eighty-five pounds and athletic but have only played golf as my exercise the past few years. We went to Hal's around one PM on Saturday and as luck would have it, Hal and I were the only men at the party, the other two neighbor's husbands were either working or out of town. So with five women and just Hal and I, it seemed like a good chance to bring up my favorite subject with Hal. After an hour of small talk and some good food and beer the women were in their own conversations and Hal suggested we go to his study and watch the pre-season football games that just started. Hal has a nice house - all the best to include his study, which was decked out with recliners and a big flat screen TV. We watched the games and small talked... Then after a few beers I got bold and asked Hal about the wild laughter I heard coming from his yard last weekend... "Sounds like someone was getting a good tickling." I said. He seemed to blush at first but then said "Oh yes, that was Sally, most ticklish woman on the planet and I love to tickle her when I can." "Oh she likes it huh?" I asked. "No, hates it, and every time I do it, I get put in the doghouse." Hal replied with a grin. "Oh that's too bad," I said. "I like tickling too and Tammi is the same way, ticklish and hates it." "Oh really, a tickler huh?" Hal asked as he looked at me with some surprise. "I have always loved tickling," says Hal. "I used to tickle all the kids in my neighborhood growing up; I was a terror," he laughed. I had noticed several times as we talked that Hal would be eyeing my size 10 feet as they sat propped up by the recliner. "I have only met a handful of people over the years that really say they like tickling." Hal intoned. "Well I'm one of them," I said, not really knowing what else to say. "Glad to know that Tom," Hal said and smiled at me as he got up and asked if I needed another beer. I agreed to the beer and as he came back in the room, he handed me my beer and then commented on my golf tan line... "Makes your feet look so white and sensitive Tom." I quickly stated (with some fear) "Not my feet," but before I could say anything else...Hal grabbed my feet in a headlock (much like he had his wife's last weekend) and said, "Oh yeah, let's see"... He scribbled his manicured nails up my soles from the heel to toes with the quickest little scratches I have ever felt...hehehhehehheheheheh, I jerked my feet, tried to kick free, and realized that Hal's grip was like a vice. "Oh Tom, they are ticklish...and soooo sensitive," he teased. "HAHAHHAHAHHAHAHA," I was laughing and struggling, not believing this was happening to me... Hal stopppp, HAHHAHAHAHAHAHHA come on, no more HAHHAHAh, no more please..."

Hal looked over his shoulder at me and said, "Oh come on Tom, you said you like tickling right"? He lightly tickled the area just above where the heel meets the sole... "HAHHAHAHAHAHHAHAHA", I screeched as my toes flexed like mad and I really tried to break free but was obviously no match for his iron grip. "Koooooottchiiiieee Kooooo," he teased as his fingers dug under my right foot toes...then my left...I was frantic, hahahhahehehehhehe, but in the same moment, felt myself getting aroused...after just a few minutes I was getting weak with laughter and realized I had a growing erection. Hal was indeed and expert tickler and taunter... "Does this tickle Tom?" he asked as he dragged his index finger down the outside of my left sole...I squirmed and giggled like a school child...no way to escape. Hal stopped after a few minutes, but kept my feet locked in his tight grip...I pleaded. "Hal, enough man, let me go"...I was trying to conceal my bulge, but my bathing suit did not help. Hal smiled at me after noticing my hard on and simply said, "Don't worry about that Tom - I could tell you were going to be ticklish the minute those flip flops hit the ground and your pink soles were exposed. You see Tom, I love to tickle, men, women, I don't care...I want to hear people laugh...and the feet are usually my first stop...but I like to tickle all over...and I think you need a tickling from head to toes..."

My mouth went dry...I didn't know what to say...here I was 38 years old, my feet trapped under the grip of a tickling mad man...and I could not get free...and I was sporting a nice hard on. "Alright Hal, enough of this... (I tried to sound firm) let me go now!" "Oh tough guy now huh Tom? You really want me to stop huh?" Before I could answer Hal started to again scribble up and down my soles with a new feverish attempt to drive me crazy...I howled instantly...STOOOOPPPPP, HHHAHAHHA...after two minutes of this torment Hal let up again...but still my feet were trapped...Now I was reduced to begging... "Hal come on, enough, please... "Hey Tom, what if I get the ladies down here to see me tickle you?" "No HAL", I was now embarrassed. "Come on Hal, my wife, I mean, don't do that..." "Ok Tom, but lets talk seriously here...If I think you are being up front with me...I'll let you go," Hal said sternly. But if not, the tickling will start again he said this with my feet still trapped between his grip. "So, you don't like to be tickled?" he asked me. "No," I quickly stated... Hal's fingers scribbled under my toes...No really...HAHHAHHAHAHH STOPPPPP, hehehhehehehheee HAL NOOOO, hahhahahahhaa." I babbled as he tickled for another minute... "You got a nice hard on and you don't like being tickled?  Or is it just a fact that a man has you in his control?" he asked me, sounding wicked. I was weak and knew a wrong comment here would be dealt with quickly... "OK, I love tickling...always have been a closet tickle freak." I stated.  I was embarrassed by the revelation but Hal just smiled and said, "Oh I know Tom, I can tell ticklee from a tickler.  I noticed you last weekend spying on the wife and I." He started to lightly stroke my soles with his index finger...I squirmed..."Hal, I wasn't spying," I began...and his fingers dug into my heels... "OH NO...hehehheheh ehahahhahahahh stoppppp OKOKOK. I was spying...please hehehehhehehee" I was weak with laughter and no strength left to fight back...Hal looked at me and told me to stay put or else...he let me go and my first thought was to run...but to where, my wife and tell her that I was being tickled to death by our neighbor?...and how would I explain the hard on?  I sat with wide eyes as Hal opened up his closet door and grabbed some soft rope he had hanging on the coat hanger. "Hal, what are you doing... come on man," I said...I started to try get off the recliner, but Hal was quick... he pinned my arms over my head as he straddled my torso...his weight was too much and all I could do was sit there as he quickly tied my hands together over my head...then in one motion and over my protest...he secured another piece to my bound hands and as he jumped off the recliner...he moved behind the chair and secured it somewhere below the recliner.  I was really scared at this point...I had no idea what would happen next...Here I am...hands tied over my head, pulled behind the chair securely bound...Hal then grabbed my swim trunks and pulled them off in one motion...now I was only wearing my tank top and naked from the waist down...I protested even stronger...not caring if anyone heard me... "HELP HELP"...but Hal grabbed a scarf from the closet and stuffed it into my mouth...mmmhhhhmmmmm was all I could mutter... he then grabbed my ankles and securely wrapped them tight with some more soft rope...securing them to the base of the chair.  I was stretched out pretty well...my erection bouncing as I struggled against my bonds...I kept thinking that my wife and neighbors would come walking in any minute... Hal said I'll be right back...and left the room...

Five minutes later Hal entered and said for me not to worry, the women wanted to do some shopping downtown and decided to go out the rest of the afternoon.  "They asked if we would like to join them, but I told them I had you all tied up down here and wouldn't be able to join them," Hal said. "They all laughed, as if I was joking…" I could hear the women getting into the cars and driving off as Hal pulled up a chair next to me. Hal produced a long stiff white feather, which he told me he intended to use on my stiff cock…and then he produced three separate paint brushes…different sizes he stated with each one producing a different effect. My eyes were wide with fear and I wanted to scream as Hal removed my gag…but I knew I was trapped. Hal opened my beer and allowed me a nice drink (I really needed it) and told me quite confidently that he was not going to hurt me…I was relieved for a moment, but then Hal told me that he was going to turn me into his personal tickling bitch…His look was so stern, but said with a slight smile, that I was actually again getting turned on… "Hal, come on, let me go, and I'll say nothing to anyone," I pleaded…Hal gave me an annoyed look and said, "What would you say…that this guy Hal, tied me up, tickled me to no ends…the same guy who owns ten plumbing companies in town…earns over 1 million dollars a year, has tied me up and tickled me for hours? Come on Tom, you are going to get tickled like never before…and when this is over…you will be begging me to let you cum…and then you will take care of this,"…he pulled down his swim trunks to show off his stiff eight-inch cock. I was scared…but so turned on… I had fantasized about being submissive to men before when I was in college going through initiations but never dreamed I would ever experience it.

I tried to protest…but Hal put up a finger to make a shhhh sound… and then used the stiff white feather to slowly trace the bottom of my shaft…I moaned…giggled…as the feather made it's way over my balls…"Like that huh?" He then used each paintbrush to work different areas of my balls and cock… The smallest brush with camel hair was used under my shaft, just below the head; the other brushes were used for similar effects. I was full of lust after ten minutes of this torment. "The ladies will be back after dinner…I told them we wanted to spend some time getting to know each other and they assured me they would not be back till seven or eight tonight…I mean Tom, its Saturday night…women have to have something to do," Hal teased…I turned my head to see that it was just after three PM in the afternoon and realized I was going to be this guy's toy for the next five hours. Hal took his time tracing the feather over my entire body…under my chin…behind my ears…it was maddening… "I love your feet Tom, masculine but soft and sooooo ticklish"…his fingers danced over my soles… "Hehhehehhehehehehhe nooooooo hehhehehehehhehehehehhehe" the tickling was driving me crazy already… "Tom are you ticklish?" he mocked as he tickled the tops of my feet which sent me into a hysterical laughter…

"HAHHAHA ewhehhehehehehehhehehehhehehehehh" was my response. "Wow Tom - your feet tops are soooo ticklish,"...he grinned and he lightly tickled over every inch of the tops of my feet...I was sweating I was laughing so hard...Hal took a break, offered me some more beer...which I took a nice big swig of...Hal downed his beer and said... "OK let's see how sensitive those armpits are huh?" He dug his cold fingers into my pits...my reaction was instant... HAHHAHHAHHAHA - I struggled so hard I thought that I could actually bust out the ropes...but my wild struggles only made me weaker and Hal's expert fingers danced down from my elbows under my biceps through my pits down to my hard nipples...After a few minutes he stopped to let me rest...but lightly rubbed my nipples as he described how he would tickle my stomach and ribs next...I got a good ten minute break as Hal made a phone call (I couldn't hear what he was saying) and finished off his beer. He sat next to me and again started to tease my cock...bringing it to full erection again...this time he put some baby oil on his hand and slowly jerked me off...each time I felt like I was getting close...he would stop...I was going nuts... "Hal, come on, let me cum... at least do that for me," I begged, not believing what I was saying... "In due time Tom... You will cum multiple times before this afternoon is done," Hal assured me. He was so assured and confident that it sent a shiver down my spine... Hal took the next minute tying my big toes together with some yarn... "Oh fuck, what are you doing now?" I asked (stupid question)...then he massaged baby oil all over my soles...heels and toes... "Tom, did you brush your teeth this morning?" he asked. "Yeah"...was my response... "How bout your feet? Did you brush them?" he asked me. "What?" I asked in shocked response. Hal then held up an electric toothbrush...smiled, turned it on and proceeded to tickle me to near death...The brush was the most ticklish thing I have ever felt...he dragged it over my soles so slowly I though I would die...he dug the device under and between my toes...maddening HHAHAHHAHHAHHAHAHAHAHha - I was screaming with laughter...I was harder then I had ever been in my life and really thought I would die when the brush found its mark over my hyper ticklish heels...NOOOOO ahhahhahahahhahahhahahahah- my head was thrashing back and forth...HALLLL Pllleasaseeee hahahahhahahahhahahha I was laughing so hard I didn't notice our neighbor Mark had come into the room and was watching with absolute amusement at my predicament. When the tickling stopped I laid there exhausted...when I opened my eyes Mark and Hal were sitting at the foot of the recliner admiring my feet. "What the hell! What are you doing here?" I asked, as I was shocked and stunned, two guys tickling me now, both neighbors of mine, what gives...I was so exhausted all I could do was quietly ask what was happening... Hal says, "Tom, you know

Mark...lives in that big house all alone... Not married... because he is gay... and also a huge foot fan like me." Mark was forty-one, handsome, a bit of a tummy, no athlete by any means, actually a computer geek with corporate ties. "Hi Tom," he smiled and as he began to massage my feet...nice toes...well kept... not a callous to be found"... He actually seemed to be studying my feet. I was so weak I couldn't even protest... Hal drank some beer, gave me a drink then started to tease my cock again...as Mark massaged my feet...Feels good Tom?" he asked me and I simply stared at him. "Answer me Tom...or I'll get out the toothbrush and find some new spots," he threatened... "Yes, it feels good"...I groaned... "Tom, from now on, when we are together, it's Yes Sir... OK... Yes sir..." my neighbor said. How could I protest... the foot massage and the hand job was driving me insane... "You want to cum?" Mark asked me. "Yes sir," I said and the stokes increased as Mark started to nibble my toes...I giggled like mad, squirmed, but instantly shot my load...my hips shook and I passed out... As I woke up I found myself being tied to Hal's downstairs bedroom bed...Four-poster bed... only sheets on the bed... I struggled as Mark and Hal pinned me to the bed... "Now now Tom... snickered Hal... "no time for that"... Mark straddled my stomach...his bulge in his shorts said he liked what was happening...and he held my arms tight to the bed and Hal used the ropes to tie me spread eagle...I really had no fight left...I was weak...exhausted actually... and couldn't believe this was happening to me... "Come on guys...let me go... I'll call the cops," I tried and they both laughed immediately and I found out why afterwards... a video camera was setup at the end of the bed... Ticklish Tom gonna call the police... What would they say down at Fidelity Bank...? Both laughed at this tease.

I was now naked, tied spread eagle, and at the hands of two of my neighbors... The phone rang and Tom went to go answer it... Mark smiled at me as he stripped down to his underwear... "Are you scared Tom?" he asked sincerely... "What do you think Mark, I barely know you, and now I'm tied to a bed, tickled and who knows what else,"...I must have sounded scared... "We aren't going to hurt you; Hal is just a fun guy who likes to take charge. A few months back his wife went to Paris with some friends... Hal invited me over and he must have noticed how much I was staring has his feet... so he wrestled me down...tied my hands behind my back and tickled me till I told him what I really wanted, which was to service his feet. I have been his foot bitch ever since. I give him massages at least once a week and also give him the best head he has ever had. He also ties me up and tickles me whenever he gets the urge, which I don't mind, but now you might be taking him from me since you are sooooo ticklish..." Mark tickled my right foot with his fingers as he watched my reaction... heehhehehehhehehee stop stop it hehehehheehh my head rolled back and forth as the tickling became more intense... "Ticklish Tom - I have admired you since the home party the neighborhood held for you last September... your feet were so hot in those flip-flops... but you barely noticed me..." Mark said and crawled onto the bed between my legs and lightly tickled the spot between my shaft and balls ever so lightly...my hips tried to move to increase the pressure, but Mark was onto that and started to tickle the outside hips... I groaned some more... Hal walked into the room, still on the phone... "You sure honey... I don't think Tom would mind, but let me get him and his wife can ask him... he is getting a beer hang on," Hal was saying as he came over to me with the phone. "This is your chance," Hal said as he covered the phone with his hand... "Tell the wife you have been taken prisoner and need her to call police... you see the ladies want to stay downtown at one of the high rise Hotels, my treat of course, and Tammi wants to make sure its ok with you. Here is your chance... but if you do this... we will tickle and torment you until they get back... then distribute the video all over town..." Hal put the phone to my ear... "Hey honey, I'm fine, you gonna stay downtown tonight (I sounded desperate I think) oh no, that's fine...I'm alright, just been laughing it up here with Hal... Yeah, he is a great guy..." Mark started to lightly tickle my balls again... (GULP) "Yeah honey, its fine, you can stay with them..." Hal started to trace a fingernail over my left armpit... "Hhehehehee" - I giggled... "No, Hal was just making fun of me..." more tickling... "Hhhheeee. "What are you guys doing?" Tammi asked sounding amused... "Oh he just walked by and tickled my foot...that's all..." Tammi then says to me... "Oh really, well how do you like it, does it tickle?" she laughed ...The light strokes from Mark were driving me insane... he had started to jerk me off...ever so lightly, but I could hardly contain myself...He used his thumb to rub my sensitive head...I'm gonna cum while I'm talking to my wife on the phone and she will know is all I can think... "Yeah ok honey; well here is Hal he wants to talk to you... bye love you..." As Hal took the phone from my ear Mark picked up the pace and within seconds I shot my load... "Hhhmmmm," I groaned... I heard Hal ask Tammi, about tickling... "Oh, he doesn't like to get tickled but he likes to tickle you?" They both laughed... "Well Tammi, I'll just have to teach him a lesson with that..." More laughter from Hal... "Oh yeah, you don't mind me tickling him then... you are so funny Tammi. Well got to run...ball game is about to start... See you guys tomorrow..."

"Is that awesome or what?" Hal asked me mockingly... "Your wife is having a blast with my wife and they are just becoming the best of friends..." Hal sat down next to me as Mark cleaned up the mess he started, namely my cum...My mind is in a fog...I've cum twice in the past thirty minutes... surely this has got to be it... "OK guys, we've had our fun... let me go now...and I'll say nothing," is all I can put together... Mark and Hal exchange an amused look at each other. "Tom, the ladies will be out all night...we are going to be together all night... Don't you get it?" Hal asked me. They both broke out into peals of laughter..."Guys, I got to go to the bathroom..." I said my first attempt at escape... "No problem Tom. Let's untie him," Hal said and as a team both neighbors untied me... then they meanly retied my hands behind my back... "Here Tom, how about a shower, that way we you can take a leak and get cleaned up all at once..." Hal suggested. I tried to disagree, but I was quickly pushed into the warm shower that Hal had started... but then surprised even more as Mark joined me in the shower... as I relieved myself... and started to soap up my back...legs... he was then on his knees with my now stiff shaft inches from his face... "Tom, can I do anything for you while I'm here?" he asked with a smirk. "No Mark...not for me..." I said a bit too smugly for Mark's taste... "Oh really...just so you know, you will be tickled and teased all night... and the only way out is to give us each a nice BJ." "What? You can't make me..." I babbled and Mark started stroking me again with a soapy hand and started to lick and nibble on my neck...I got mad and tried to push him off, but his size kept me pinned... he tweaked my nipples and I became very aroused but not wanting to show my eagerness for Mark to continue his erotic play... Hal then came to the shower and said "Times up Mark... lets get him dried off and get that body tied and tickled again..."

I was surprised this time as Hal and Mark tied me face down with my feet hanging over the edge of the bed... "My how vulnerable you are right now," teased Mark..."You know Tammi told me how ticklish you are and that once in college your roommate's tied you to your bed and tickled your feet till you peed your pants...is that true?" My gosh I thought, I had almost forgotten that... we were all drunk and they would not stop tickling me till I peed myself... "Well I'm gonna tickle you from head to toes...and won't stop till you beg me to let you give me a BJ... I know you are not into it... but that's the only way you are going to get me to stop... I need a tickle toy, Mark is fun, but not really into it like you are and besides your feet are sooooo HOT huh Mark?" Mark has already started to lick my soles from the balls of my foot up to my heels... Being face down he licks my feet like a Popsicle stick. I'm already squirming as Hal starts to lightly tickle down my sides...hehehhehehehhe no

Hal, NOOO PLLEASEEE lahhahahahhah. "Why didn't you tell the wife what was happening to you Tom, that was your chance right?" HAHHAHAH ppllleasee I don't know why, hehehhehehhe ahahhahahahahah. "Is it because you wanted this to happen?" "NO!" I said too quickly and Hal picked up the tickling, digging his fingers into my pits from behind while laying on my back...His stiffness was pressing down on my lower back and I could tell Hal was ready to go...After a minute he stopped tickling me and asked Mark to stop licking my feet. He lay next to me and asked if I would give him some relief...I was exhausted and eyeing his large cock I imagined how impossible it would be to get that down...I meekly said, "I can do it with my hand..." "Wrong answer Tom..." he pointed to Mark and said, "Get the baby oil and toothbrush from the study please." Mark answered with a yes sir, and took off down the hallway. Tom you don't get it do you...the video camera is rolling and I can edit it to look like anything..." Mark came into the room and Hal commanded him to spread the baby oil all over my soles and tickle them until he got some relief...Within a minute the toothbrush was humming itself over my soles...I screamed and shook with such raucous laughter that I thought I would die. Five minutes later Hal stopped Mark, and untied my left hand from the corner post so that only my legs and right arm were tied... He positioned himself next to my head and his eight inch cock was purple and ready to explode. "Anytime you want to relieve me - just let me know..." he pointed to Mark and the tickling picked up again...Mark dug the brush under my toes, very slowly, smoothly gliding under each digit...I knew I would lose my mind...after a few minutes of intense tickling Mark stopped and crawled up the bed next to me and started to lightly tickle my back... I was soooo aroused and Hal was smiling at me that I finally gave in and started to work over his large cock...I could barely fit it, but after a few tries it got easier and after a minute Hal was shooting his load over me and the bed. "MMMMMMMMM - good one Tom... Not bad for a first timer..." he said. I was a bit humiliated but still very turned on...Mark sensed this and untied my feet and other arm...I laid between my neighbors and as I played with Hal's cock, Mark gave me a BJ that again, made me pass out... I don't know how long I was out, but when I woke up, Mark was tied to the bed with his big feet hanging over the edge and a note left next to him from Hal saying...you get two hours to tickle him to your hearts content... then I get to tickle both of you... A smile crept across my face as I realized I had found a true friend in Hal...as I lay over Mark's legs and positioned myself over his size twelve feet ... I was going to like my new neighbors...HAHHAHAHHA, Mark howled as I dug my fingers into his soles...

# TIMMY'S CHRISTMAS PRESENT

## Written by: Timmy Backman

T'was Christmas morning and all through the house rang the laughter and guffawing of Timmy B...the "master?" of his domain! He was naked, you see, bare as the prize goose ready for the Cratchet's oven. He was trussed up too, and splayed out like the dissected frog in your high school biology class. Unwrapping this present had been his biggest mistake of the whole holiday... for you see this present was to be a Christmas tickling to last until after New Years...A week of tickle torture at the hands and instruments of all his tickle buddies...that just might be the complete undoing of poor Timmy Backman.

While visions of sugarplums danced in other's heads, Timmy had visions of tickle insanity dancing in his. Once he had read the note in the brightly colored envelope and had uttered once more "Oh NO!" he was set upon by his holiday gathering of tickle buddies and buddettes. There was Vince and Christopher Trevor of course. But, then they were joined by his lovely wife Stephanie, her friend Valerie, Valerie's assistant Douglas, Christopher's alter ego Ronald Greene, Mr. Wang and his assistant Makya Leekalot, Makya's husband Sir Leekalot, Bull from the Leather Bar and a bunch of the leather clad guys, plus a host of others who were eager and willing to make this Timmy's most ticklish Christmas of all...and not just Christmas but to extend it all the way through New Year's Eve.

Stephanie had gathered this group of tickle torturers to give Timmy the most intense and longest tickle session he had ever experienced. She loved her husband but she dearly loved to tickle him and it was a real turn on for her to see others tickle him too. Over the years she had discovered some of the ticklish predicaments Timmy had gotten into. She had actually participated in some. Stephanie was not the jealous type and knew that Timmy was true to her. It was just part of his ticklish weakness that caused his sexual excitement. So, she was not angry when he had an orgasm(s) as a result of being tickle tortured.

So, the tickle buddies gathered at Timmy and Stephanie's house... Timmy was extremely nervous to see them all together. And, once he opened his envelope, they set on him...stripped him and held him splayed out in four directions. Timmy was tickled with fingers and feathers, brushes and bristles, just all kinds of things. He was tickled around his neck, up and down his arms, in his armpits, on his belly and sides, up and down his bare legs, and also those most sensitive spots. Someone held mistletoe over his chest which resulted in puckered lips on each nip...but teeth and tongue also worked their magic on those nips. Fingers and feathers and brushes worked up and down his bare feet up and down each sole and in, around and in between each toe.

Timmy was laughing and screaming at the fun everyone was having at his expense. His cock had sprung to full attention and was waving around like a swishing antenna and beginning to leak clear liquid from his piss slit. It was only Christmas Eve and Timmy knew that he would be stark raving insane if this lasted through New Year's Eve.

Then...probably Vince or Ronald or both began to play his rumbling balls and cock with stiff feathers. On top of the tickling, this was really maddening. They teased his cock and balls until he was on the verge of blowing his cum all over...but they measured his teasing to keep him poised there for a while. Timmy was screaming for relief when one of them attacked his asshole with a stiff pointy feather...spinning it in his anus. This was too much for the laddy and he squirted his thick, white goo like a geyser. As his balls pumped his cum out the end of his dick, a cheer went up from the gathering and they doubled their tickle efforts...which finally drove the boy to unconsciousness.

Timmy's collapse gave everyone a break and a chance to plan the remainder of his week long tickle torture present.

Holy shit!

# BIRTHDAY SUIT

## Written by: Dutch Roberts

"Yeah, Raf, you're gonna have to tell me the rest over dinner tonight and I want to hear every last succulent detail, but, I have to run, someone's at the door," Perry informed his friend, on the other end of the line, as he made his way down the hallway, from kitchen to foyer. "No, I have no idea who it is. I'll catch you later," he concluded, as he ran a hand over the ebony-colored, perfectly tied bow at his neck.

Flipping his cell phone closed and sliding it into an interior pocket of his crisp, white dinner jacket Perry approached the front door and twisted the gold knob. Swinging it open he found himself, to his utter surprise, face-to-face with two lean, leather-clad strangers. Swiftly, they forced their way in, each taking a hold of an arm as they made their way back up the hallway, toward the kitchen, only pausing long enough to kick the front door closed.

"What the fuck!" Perry bellowed, struggling to break free of their strong hold.

"Quiet," the one to his right barked through his leather mask with a tinge of metal in his voice.

"Yeah, shut the hell up," the second one commanded through his narrow mouth slit, in a similar electronically modified voice.

They moved quickly through the kitchen to the sound of Perry's patent leather shoes clicking upon the tiled floor. Their soft leather boots made no noise at all. Again he called out, "What the fuck do you want?" However, the two remained silent this time as they purposefully made their way for the basement door located at the back of the spacious room.

It instantly struck Perry that they knew exactly where they were taking him. They had a specific destination. But how could they know? Who were these guys?

With little fanfare, the three made their way down to the dark, unfurnished basement. A slight smell of mildew washed over them as they descended. The darkness nearly engulfed them, until one of the punks whipped out a flashlight.

"Through there," the one directed the other with a narrow beam of light.

"Who the hell are you two?" Perry questioned, ducking his head below several pipes as they made their way toward a pile of cardboard boxes neatly tucked into a corner.

"Here, you hold him. I'll get rid of these," the more aggressive of the two informed the other.

Helplessly, Perry watched as the guy moved into action, quickly disposing of the pile – the pile that usually worked to cover a secret very few knew of. Soon enough, a door was revealed and, within seconds, he was being forced through that very door.

Stumbling forward, Perry quickly found himself, along with the two punks, standing in the middle of his playroom. As the lights came to life around the three men, the details of the chamber were revealed.

Positioned in the center of the room was what appeared to be an exam table, but instead of it being a stark metal contraption, this one was covered in thick, leather pads, which matched the generous padding on the walls. To the right of the table was situated a plush, crimson-colored, velvet covered chair. However, this was no ordinary piece of furniture as the arms and legs both had leather restraints attached to them and the high back had a head strap. To the left of the table was a far more unusual piece of equipment – a leather covered stock, very similar to the ones used in less civilized times. With a space for both wrists and ankles to be captured, the contraption held the rapt attention of both intruders, until the leader pulled his gaze away and redirected it toward Perry.

"Well, Mr. Richards, you seem to have all the right toys for us to have a rather enjoyable evening together," he noted as he moved closer to the formally attired man. "Although, I'm guessing you were heading somewhere pretty special to begin with?" he continued as he proceeded to run a gloved hand over the sleeve of Perry's tuxedo jacket.

Pulling away, Perry remained silent as he attempted to figure out who these guys were.

*Christopher?*, he wondered to himself. *No*, he firmly decided. *They're both too tall. Alan?*, he thought, as he attempted to put a face to the metallic voice. *Hmmm, no, couldn't be him either*, he reasoned. *Who the hell are these guys and how do they know me so well?*

"I can see the wheels turning, Mr. Richards, but it's no use. You'll never guess who we are, but, I will tell you this, you're going to know what it's like to be handled by us all too well."

Perry, unnerved by this statement, made a bold attempt to bolt from the room, but he was quickly forced back in as the two took a hold of him and flung him, rather roughly, into the velvet chair. Within a matter of seconds he was firmly strapped into place as each punk worked his wrists into the padded fetters. Oddly enough, they didn't utilize the ankle restraints.

"You can't do this!" he howled, bucking and kicking wildly.

"Uh, yeah, we can," the punk to his left calmly noted.

"Just watch us," the second added.

As Perry continued to thrash about, the two punks proceeded to walk the room, searching through the closets, cabinets and dressers situated around the perimeter. With each door flung open and every drawer slid out, more and more erotic paraphernalia came into view. Whips, paddles, ball-gags, butt-plugs, dildos, nipple clamps, blindfolds and feather ticklers were just a few of the items found among the veritable treasure trove of toys.

"Damn, you've really thought of it all!" one assailant exclaimed as he took a riding crop into his gloved hand.

"Fuck. Just look at all this gear too," the other added as he opened the last closet, exposing hanger after hanger of leather vests, pants and jackets.

"Jeez. Now that's a collection to be proud of," the crop-wielding punk added. "But, I can't help wonder, why is it all hidden down here?"

Once again, Perry became tight lipped, as a flash of anger played across his handsome face. How dare they invade his home and his private space this way!

"Aw, come now, there has to be a good reason as to why this is all neatly tucked away... right?" the crop wielder continued to question as he waved the implement through the air.

"I don't think he's going to answer you," his accomplice noted as he slid into a thick, leather trench coat he pulled from the closet.

"Well, then, perhaps we need to coax it out of him...through any means possible."

Perry, feeling his body tense up within his impeccably tailored tuxedo, started to genuinely worry about where this situation was going. The posturing of each leather-clad punk made him firmly believe that they meant business. They clearly intended to utilize the room to its fullest extent, which worried him greatly. He knew what could be done in this room. He'd done it all before. Would they really go that far?

"Listen, guys, there's no need to force the situation. Why don't we try to relax and enjoy..."

CRACK!

The lash of a whip came out of nowhere and in a flash it made contact with the left leg of Perry's dress pants. Slicing through the smooth fabric, the tongue of the tool managed not to draw blood, which clearly demonstrated the skill of the person using it.

"Fuck!" Perry cried out, bucking violently as a response to the unexpected whipping.

"There's more where that came from, my friend," the whip-wielding punk purred through his mask. "However, we're not really here to whip and beat the living daylights out of you, we're here to show you a great time! We've come to satisfy your every whim and desire, to the best of our ability. It is your birthday after all."

Startled by this confession, Perry shook his head in disbelief. Clearly, they were toying with him, lulling him into a false sense of security...or were they?

"That's right, Mr. Richards, we're going to take you on a wild ride and it starts...NOW!"

With that, the whip flew through the air once more and continued to splice through the delicate fabric of Perry's trousers. In a flash, the tool rendered the left leg useless as the severed material came undone, sliding down and pooling around his ankle, exposing the over-the-calf, silk sock found within. In a matter of seconds, the right leg was joining it in its demise.

Crouching before Perry, the crop-wielding punk tugged at the two pieces of fabric until they came free, completely exposing his legs from mid-thigh down. With a surprisingly gentle hand the punk then stroked the exposed skin, brushing the delicate hairs on Perry's legs ever so softly, which sent a visible chill through his body almost immediately.

"Excellent," the whip-wielder purred as he moved closer and knelt, joining his partner in the act.

Slowly, the two danced their fingers across the exposed flesh until finally they each took one of Perry's highly polished shoes and removed it. Soon enough his silk encased feet were free of the leather accessories. They were free to be methodically massaged and carefully caressed. Free to be tenderly toyed with and softly stroked, over, and over, and over again.

Perry, unable to fight the overpowering sensation that was coursing through his body, began – much to his chagrin – to giggle.

As the delightful sound filled the chamber, the two punks proceeded to perform their task with even greater exuberance.

"Please...oh God! You're...driving me...WILD!" Perry exclaimed, between fits of laughter, with tears of elation in his eyes.

With this exclamation, the two abruptly stopped, as Perry continued to snicker.

Standing, the two punks made their way toward a nearby dresser. Perry watched as they fished through the toys found within. As he waited for their next assault, he suddenly realized that he was not only far more relaxed – in regard to his predicament – but also very aroused, as his cock sprang to life in his cotton boxer briefs.

*Who are these guys?*, his mind questioned for the second time. *How do they fuckin' know so much about me? Very few know about my foot fetish, and even fewer know how much I love a good tickling.*

"Ok, Mr. Richards, it's time to ramp up the excitement quota just a bit," one of the punks noted as he approached with a leather blindfold in his hand.

"Yeah, you being able to see what's coming takes some of the fun out of this," the second guy added. "Don't ya think?"

Perry, feeling slightly more comfortable in the situation, simply nodded in agreement. For some strange reason he began to believe these punks when they said they were here to bring him nothing but pleasure. Perhaps it was the nagging feeling that he somehow knew them, which was only natural, since they seemed to know far too much about him. The one currently standing to his right, in particular, seemed vaguely familiar, but he couldn't put his finger on it just yet.

"Why did you have to ruin my pants?" Perry suddenly found himself questioning. "Do you have any idea how much this garment cost?"

"Well, here's a more important question, Mr. Richards," the blindfold toting punk began, "do you really think we give a shit?"

With that the two punks began to laugh and as they continued to snicker each one pounced on Perry. Swiftly the blindfold was placed over his eyes, plunging him into darkness. Immediately his other senses became heightened, as he felt smooth, leather-clad hands running all over his body. Piece by piece his beautiful tuxedo was torn from his form. The sound of fabric shredding filled the small, padded chamber, as each layer was forcibly removed. Surprising himself, Perry didn't protest and allowed this to happen. Did he really have a choice? Besides, the sound of the fabric ripping was causing his cock and balls to stir wildly in his shorts.

First, he could feel them working on his perfectly tailored dinner jacket. In his minds eye he could see one of them tugging at the shawl collar, snapping the meticulous stitches that held it in place, while the other tore at his breast pocket, sending the crimson-colored, silk square held within to the floor. This was followed by each of them working on a sleeve, starting at the shoulder and ripping their way down to his bound wrists, until both were removed and discarded. The body of the jacket was last and it took several hard tugs to get it off of him, since the silk lining was well crafted, but soon enough it too was added to the growing pile of rags forming at his feet.

Next they worked on his dark, four-button vest, as well as what was left of his pants, shredding each piece away. With great ease, highly polished buttons and a sparkling, silver zipper was sent soaring through the air. Soon enough they would have him down to his tight cotton undershirt and boxer briefs. However, his impeccable dress shirt would need to be dealt with first.

As the two moved to work on this particular item, their hands began to slow in their progression, exploring and caressing the body held within. Their fingers lingered on his nipples, toying and tweaking the mini bumps until they became fully erect below the surface of the dress shirt, which elicited a slight moan from their owner. Next, they each traced a line down the side of the garment, then slowly back up, until each found his way into Perry's armpit. Soon, though, they made their way around and traced the line of the seam found at the shoulder, working their way down to the thick, French cuffs. Each punk let his fingers gracefully dance over the smooth fabric, until their fingers found the chunky silver and diamond links placed at Perry's wrists, just below the restraints.

Perry, relishing their touch, continued to grow hard in his cotton shorts. He became so erect that the tip of his throbbing manhood began to poke out from behind the elastic waistband. The more they handled him, the harder he became, until a thick stream of pre started to ooze out of his throbbing tool.

"Almost there," one of the punks muttered as he popped the expensive link from the stiff cuff and took a firm hold of the sleeve attached. Within seconds it too was vanquished, exposing Perry's muscular arm within. Ripping and tugging, the punks swiftly removed what was left of the once flawless dress shirt, adding it to pile on the floor.

Standing, both leather boys took a good, hard look at their nearly naked captive and then one of them muttered, "Damn, what a shame we had to destroy his pretty clothes, but orders are orders after all."

"Shhh," the second punk hissed.

Hearing this, Perry perked up, suddenly realizing that the two punks were on some sort of assignment, on behalf of someone else – someone who apparently knew him very well.

*Raf? Alex? Who put these punks up to this?* Perry thought as he sat waiting for the two of them to continue with their 'torture.' No matter who was behind this they were both cruel and, in a way, very kind.

"Hmm, that looks like a smile on his lips," one of the punks took note.

"Yeah, but he's not going to be simply smiling for very long because he'll be uncontrollably laughing by the time we're finished with him," the second punk replied. "What we did to his feet a few minutes ago was just a drop in the bucket."

Perry's cock suddenly bucked inside of his tight boxers, drooling even more pre, so much so that his crotch was now soaked in the crystal-clear fluid.

"Damn, look at that! We haven't even started and he's on the verge of spewing his hot load."

"Wow. I think you're right."

The two leisurely approached Perry. Quietly they circled, not laying a finger on him, building the tension and suspense of the moment. They watched as he shifted in his seat, obviously growing impatient with them or...was he itching with desire for them to start? It was a little hard to tell at this point. The two assailants were fully aware of what their captive desired, but was he going to be a willing participant from beginning to end? If they were mind readers they would know exactly how to proceed, although, truth told, the man who hired them gave them a pretty good idea of what needed to be achieved here.

As Perry's mind flooded with all of the erotic possibilities this situation held, a gentle, almost feather-soft caress occurred along his left shoulder, glided up along the side of his neck, brushed the tips of the hairs found there and ended just behind his earlobe. Responding immediately, a shiver coursed through Perry's entire body. Then, he felt something wet and warm – a tongue – slide into his ear cavity and gently flick at the sensitive bumps and ridges found there. This simple gesture drove Perry utterly insane, causing him to writhe in his bindings. However, in an instant it was over.

"No...don't...stop," Perry muttered between light-hearted chuckles and downright giggles.

Within seconds, Perry felt yet another subtle caress. This time it started on the edge of one pectoral and trailed its way across to the other, toying with his nipples along the way, which were quickly growing erect within his smooth, cotton undershirt. Then, in an instant, this came to a halt as well; however he didn't have to wait too long for another bout of tender fondling to begin.

The lines of his body were lightly traced. His exposed flesh was gingerly worked, drawing the hairs on his arms and legs to their full attention. Goosebumps appeared all over his toned muscles. His body quickly became fully charged, relishing every subtle stroke applied by the two punks.

"Oh, God," Perry moaned, "that feels...amazing!"

The two assailants continued working their captive's body until they mutually decided to relocate him to one of the other two devices found in the chamber. The chair, while entertaining, was too confining to achieve their ultimate goal.

It was time to get serious.

Feeling their hands upon his bound wrists, Perry swiftly found himself freed, brought to his feet and directed across the room. As he walked, he could feel what was left of his tuxedo below his socked feet. He imagined the torn and shredded pieces getting mashed into the floor. He nearly slipped on what was left of the silk lining to his dinner jacket.

*The table,* he found himself pondering, almost as a distraction, *or the stock? Please let it be the stock they put me in!*

Then, to his mild surprise, he felt their leather encased hands on his body, stripping him of his undershirt and boxers, leaving him completely exposed, save his silk encased feet. His erect, drooling tool darted out in all its glory, bouncing freely in the air above his succulent, smooth sac. A copious stream of pre leaked out and splattered upon the tiled floor, loud enough for all three men to hear.

"Damn, this guy is going to erupt like a volcano!"

"Ok, let's get him into position."

Moving Perry into place, the two punks soon had him safely secured in the leather stock, with his ankles bound and his feet left dangling – dangling freely, prone to any and all assaults.

"Please...I beg you, take full advantage of this situation," Perry moaned as his pulse quickened and his breathing became more labored.

"Fuck, this is almost too easy," one punk exclaimed as he moved into position, removing his gloves along the way.

"Yeah, way too easy," the second agreed as he knelt across from his cohort, removing his gloves as well.

Slowly, with great ease, the two began to stroke Perry's ankles. Their nimble, bare fingers danced upon his silk covered skin. They traced the smooth hills and valleys, covering every inch. They hovered, just far enough above, so that only the very tips of their fingers made contact. After several passes, Perry began to moan and even shudder a bit. It was simply intoxicating the way they expertly handled him.

"Yes, that's it...toy with me," he sputtered between chuckles. "Tease me."

The two continued, increasing the amount of pressure they applied, tracing their nails across the sheer silk fabric, which sent waves of pleasure through Perry's entire body, causing him to first chuckle and then laugh!

"OH GOD! YES!" he cried, curling his toes, as they swiftly moved from the tops of his feet to the ever-so-sensitive undersides.

Stroking Perry's soles, each punk was relentless in his handling of the man's feet. Repeatedly they ran a finger up and down, from his toes to his heels. They moved in zigzags, circles and direct lines, alternating between each, as well as changing the amount of pressure they applied. Occasionally a finger was replaced with the use of a tongue, which only made the action all that more erotic and desirable.

"OH FUCK!" Perry screamed as he bucked in his restraints, flailing his arms wildly, shaking the entire stock.

They continued to passionately molest his feet, feeding off of his uproarious laughter, until one of them decided to kick the situation up another notch. Standing, the trench coat wearing punk abandoned his partner in crime

– who remained in place, working on Perry's feet – and quickly made his way to one of the many cabinets that held the array of naughty toys and tools. Returning, he moved into place at the other end of the stock and, without much warning, took a hold of Perry's left wrist and then his right. With great skill the punk bound him in a satin rope, then, after tossing it over an exposed beam, tugged his arms over his head, completely exposing his armpits.

"Oh no...please...you can't! You wouldn't! Not my feet *and* my...," but Perry was unable to finish his sentence because immediately his underarms were assaulted. The thick, silken hairs found within his vulnerable pits were soon tussled, fondled and gingerly toyed with, sending waves of ecstasy through his body.

The two punks continued, one on each end, sending Perry into an absolute, uncontrollable frenzy. Once more they alternated the patterns they traced over his skin, as well as the pressure they applied. At times their movements were subtle and light, nearly nonexistent, while at other times they were more intense and far more potent. They could have used any number of implements found in the chamber, but, instead, they selected to employ their bare hands, as well as their tongues, which was far more effective.

"You're...driving me...to the edge!" Perry bellowed, with tears of joy streaming down his cheeks, as he continued to thrash in the stock. It took a mere glance at his gyrating cock and tight balls to see that he was indeed drawing close to spewing a torrent of seed. The punks were more than willing to bring the situation to its ultimate climax. At this point they had been working on the man for several hours. Could he really take much more of this?

The delicious answer to such a simple question was promptly provided.

"DEAR GOD!" was the final exclamation uttered by the bound – albeit euphoric – man as his entire body went ramrod straight in its restraints. Jutting his hips up and tossing his head back, Perry's cock was thrust into the air just as he launched his thick, copious, sizzling load. The first abundant spray of jizz soared and proceeded to rain down upon the punk at his feet. The second washed over his own sweat soaked body, as the third was feasted on by the trench coat wearing punk from above.

Taking their leave, only after undoing Perry's restraints, the two punks made their way out of the chamber, as well as the house, without another word spoken. Their task was complete and there was no need to linger.

Perry, relishing in the moment, was startled when his cell phone went off. Standing, he quickly moved to the tattered remains of his dinner jacket and withdrew the device from what was left of the interior pocket.

"Hello," he simply stated as he brought the phone to his smirk-filled mouth.

"Perry? Where the hell are you?" his friend Raf questioned on the other end.

"I, uh, well...where do I start? It's been a *very* interesting evening," Perry began. "As a matter of fact, I had figured it was your doing."

"What the hell are you talking about? Have you started celebrating without me? Are you drunk?" Raf continued to question his friend.

"Flying high, perhaps, but drunk, no," Perry replied as he made his way out of the playroom.

"Well, you better get your lofty ass over here. I have a fantastic dinner arranged for the two of us at a rather impressive five star restaurant," Raf scolded his friend.

"I'm coming. Don't worry. Although, I may have an issue with my attire...it's safe to assume it's a black tie only establishment," Perry calmly noted as he made his way from the basement to the kitchen, completely stripped of his handsome formal wear.

"How is that possible? I know for a fact you own a tuxedo. It's a bit old, and maybe a little out of style, but it works. So don't give me that shit. You better be here within the hour, looking your best," Raf continued to scold, before abruptly disconnecting.

Perry, still riding on the waves of euphoria that rippled through his entire body, stopped dead in his tracks as he approached the front hall. There, to his left, situated in the middle of his living room was what appeared to be a tailor's bust and upon it was the most stunning garment he had ever seen with his own two eyes. Slowly approaching the formally dressed bust, his hand automatically went to the crisp envelope that was hanging from a satin ribbon around the things neck. Opening it, he removed the note found within.

*Dear P.R.,*

*If everything has gone according to plan, you should be standing before this beautifully suited bust, in, well, nothing but your birthday suit – save for your dress socks – in a state of utter bliss. I sincerely hope that my two boys handled you with great care and provided several hours of absolute pleasure. The one, in particular, was eager to get his skilled hands on you...having only toyed with you for a brief time once before.*

*As a token of my fondness for you, please accept this one-of-a-kind garment. Personally, I felt, it was time to update your wardrobe. I hope you are not offended by the way I went about achieving such a task. I thought you would be tickled – pun intended – by such a generous gesture.*

*With My Deepest Affection,*

*D.R.*

Perry, stunned into silence, read the card several more times, before quietly placing it on a nearby table. He had no clue as to who D.R. was, however, he was more than willing to play along, for the tuxedo set before him was simply stunning and the process used to bring it to him was completely captivating. As for the riddle of who the two boys were, he was rather lost there as well, although, if he had to venture a guess, he was pretty sure he would run into one of them all too soon. The next time he visited his local barber shop, he would test his theory out on a particular blond, shoeshine boy – a talented little fuck who went by the name of Billy.

# VALERIE'S SECOND SHOT AT TIMMY

## Written by: Timmy Backman

I told you that Valerie, Stephanie's friend, and I really didn't get along all that well. She's the one who gave Steph and me the Spinning Chinaman, and she had used my ticklishness, that she actually learned from Steph, to persuade me to buy an expensive desk for Steph. It was on that occasion that she tricked me into the Spinning Chinaman and proceeded to spin me dizzy and disoriented and then tickle the ever loving shit out of me until I bought the desk. She also discovered my fantasy and fetish for women's feet and legs. Now, my wife has some great feet and legs. But, Valerie...she's got the legs and feet of a dancer, which really, really, really turns me on. Now, Steph, besides knowing how ticklish I am and using it against me, she also knows about my foot fetish. She's not jealous; she really just thinks it's another funny quirk about me.

So, Steph and I went out to dinner and dancing with Valerie and one of her dates. Being a decorator, she always seems to be out with gay guys, fellow decorators. I guess neither of them is looking for anything more than just dinner, dancing, a movie, just whatever the occasion calls for. But, in the back of my mind, I really think that Valerie liked girls more than men. And I think she especially likes Stephanie. So, that sort of made us rivals. But, Valerie was sexy and she tended to use that to her advantage and she used it against me.

Douglas was Valerie's date...escort for the night. He's much like me, in that he's a very attractive, athletic guy. But, you'd never believe he was a decorator. We went to Emile's for dinner and dancing. We had a great meal, Steph and I on one side of the table and Valerie and Douglas on the other. Val was across from me and Douglas was across from Steph. We danced before dinner, Douglas and I dancing with both women. Steph commented that she actually thought Douglas was a better dancer than I. Well, I thought..."No, wonder, he's light in his loafers." We finally decided to eat and placed our orders for dinner.

Steph loves to talk and she was hogging the conversation, which left the rest of us listening or just briefly replying to her. So, Steph chattered on while we sipped our pre-dinner wine. Then I heard the soft clatter of shoes on the hard restaurant floor. When I heard that I looked at Val who was staring at me over her wine glass. Then, I felt a pair of bare feet begin to snake their way up my left pants leg. I almost choked, which made Val snicker as her bare feet, which she already knew I found very sexy, began to tickle the hair on my leg. She was running her feet alternatingly up my pants leg, all the way to my knee. Well, besides making me work to stifle a giggle, the mere thought of her sexy bare feet on my leg, not to mention the feel of her bare feet on my leg, was causing me to develop an erection.

Then to my astonishment, I felt something on my right leg. It wasn't Val, and Steph was too busy talking to us to be pre-occupied with playing footsie with me. So, if it's not Steph...and it's not Val...it could only be... Douglas? I looked over at Douglas and he was giving me the same sexy stare over his wine glass that Val was giving me.

"Oh, Shit" I said to myself "Valerie's date is coming on to me." And Douglas seemed to be just adept at stroking his leg and Val was. This not only tickled, it was maddening. My dick got even harder and the obscene notion that another man was stroking my leg under the table...and right in the presence of my wife, who obliviously talked on. Valerie and Douglas continued to work on me all during dinner. They kept teasing me and managed to keep me hard as a rock the entire meal.

Once the meal was over I told them that I would take care of the bill and for them to meet me in the lobby. This way I would be able to use my napkin to cover my obvious tent in my suit pants while Steph, Val and Douglas rose and left the table. I dragged out the bill paying process long enough for my erection to subside. Then I joined them in the lobby. Both Val and Douglas were obvious when they looked at my crotch to see if I was still erect. I thought I was safe. But, that was short lived when Steph invited Val and Douglas over to the house for drinks. I tried to divert this invitation, but Steph pooh poohed me and it was on. Since we had come in separate cars, Val and Douglas followed me and Steph to our house. Once on another occasion when I had had one too many, Steph demanded to drive and I wound up in the back seat with Douglas and Val was in the front with Steph. Well, that night, Douglas made a move on me, right there in the back seat of my own car with my wife right up front. But, that was another story.

Once we got home and the drinks got served, Valerie wanted Douglas to see the Spinning Chinaman. Val used the excuse that Douglas was a decorator like she was and this was a unique piece and he needed to see it demonstrated. Right away I objected. I always seemed to get myself prodded, persuaded, cajoled, or tricked into the Spinning Chinaman, and in the end, it was I who wound up being the brunt of everyone else's fun at my dizzy and ticklish expense. But, I wasn't going to let them do it to me this time...NO SIR-REE BOB TAIL!

Well Steph took Val's side. "Timmy, I think Douglas needs to see the Spinning Chinaman in action and you know it...he, he from the inside out... he, he (she giggled, remembering all of the past times I had been a captive of this devilish device)."

"That's not funny." I demanded. "If he wants to see the Chinaman, then he can be mounted in that...thing."

"Mounted it that thing? Hmmm!" Douglas mumbled and looked on with much more interest.

"Now Timmy," Steph turned on the charm. "You know that Douglas is a guest in our home. Plus, he needs to see it in action, not experience it. Maybe he can experience it later." Stephanie continued to be persuasive as only my beautiful wife could be.

But I was being more stubborn this time. "Ok then, Steph, you get in there and show him how it works!" I said smugly, as if I was getting the upper hand.

"OH No dear, I have on a dress, and that would be totally improper for me to get into the Chinaman while wearing a dress." Steph smirked and sipped her drink as she had once more deflected my macho attempt at taking control.

Feeling a little defeated, I turned toward Val, who was quick and was holding out the skirt of her dress as if saying, "And so am I big boy." And she smirked and sipped her drink also.

Now, beginning to recognize my defeat I found that I was allowing Steph and Val to push me toward the Spinning Chinaman. And, as they guided me there I was whining, "Why is it always me. Why do I always have to demonstrate the Chinaman?"

"Timmy dear, you do such a good job as a demonstrator. Everyone has so much fun when you demonstrate the Chinaman." Steph played on my ego as she and Val strapped my reluctant arms and legs into the frame, yet once more. Oh woe is me…

Then as they secured the waist straps, Douglas got really interested, "Wow, this looks interesting already. I can't wait to see how this works!" Douglas was grinning big time now. And his cock was stirring in his slacks as he watched the girls strap hunky me into the metal frame.

Valerie got Stephanie another drink as my wife was showing Douglas how the Spinning Chinaman worked and how we usually played question games…how wrong or slow answers result in spinning. I whooped and hollered as Stephanie gave him some demonstration spins, first round and round and then head over heels. Stephanie, Valerie and Douglas laughed and clinked glasses and drank away as poor me spun away.

Valerie then asked Stephanie to refresh her drink…she really did this to get Steph out of the room so she could have a little shot at teasing me plus, letting Douglas know just how ticklish I really am.

Stephanie left the room...walking a little unsteady, since she'd had more than her usual. With Steph out of the room, Val kicked off her shoes and flipped me to an upside down position in the frame. Then, against my protests, she began rubbing her bare feet on my face, one at a time. It took but seconds and she could see the results, a growing tent in my pleated pants. As Val enjoyed this power over me, she told Douglas that I was extremely ticklish. And that I almost don't have a spot that's not ticklish. Douglas's eyes lit up. Now, Val was not only content with teasing poor me with her bare feet, but she began to massage my stiffy right through my pleated pants. I am true to my wife, as best as I can be, but I am extremely weak when it comes to pretty feet and Vals definitely fit that category. I quit complaining and began licking at Vals luscious tootsies and I moaned as she started rubbing my manhood. I swear I really could not help myself.

Hearing Stephanie coming back, Val whispered to Douglas, "Stephanie and I are going to go try on clothes and do some other girl things. So, you stay here and play with Timmy! And, by the way, you might also substitute stripping for spinning in the Chinaman. So, you just might be able to get Timmy boy here naked." And she winked at Douglas.

Well, Douglas was more than happy to have the studly, tied up, sexually stimulated and supposedly ticklish me to play with.

"Steph honey!" Valerie said as Stephanie came back into the room... weaving slightly from her intoxication. "Didn't you tell me you got some new lingerie recently?" Valerie gave Timmy one last brush with her foot and moved to meet Stephanie. Val took her drink and turned Stephanie around. "Now, what was it you bought?" guiding her out of the room and toward the bedroom. With me occupied...and she was sure that Douglas would keep poor me occupied for a good long while...she would have a chance of getting into Stephanie's panties. Just maybe.

"Oh, I'd love to show you what I bought. But, Timmy is still in the Chinaman and I hate to leave Douglas...he's a guest in my home." Steph said, looking back over her shoulder in the direction of us two guys. I was still licking my lips and thinking about Val's feet. And Douglas was closing in on me in the Spinning Chinaman, investigating how he was going to enjoy this evening.

"Oh, the guys are alright. Timmy is showing Douglas the Chinaman and I know that Douglas has LOTS of questions to quiz Timmy with. So, show me your stuff." Val said and directed Stephanie out of the room, the two of them sipping their drinks as they walked to the bedroom. "Didn't you tell me you got this stuff at Victoria's Secret?" Clinking glasses with Stephanie, "Cheers, Here's to sexy lingerie!" and she pushed Steph's glass toward her lips and Steph drank.

Stephanie giggled as she was directed down the hall sipping on her drink. "Yes! They really have some HOT stuff. Timmy really gets churned up when I put on my VS outfits. Hee hee!"

"I'd like to see them. Maybe I could try some on? Hey, we both could try on outfits...sort of like a little private fashion show. What do you say, Steph? It'll be fun." Valerie insisted and was being persuasive and Steph was weakened by alcohol.

"OK!" Stephanie giggled. "Yeah, that would be fun." So, Valerie's little plan was falling into place. I was strapped into the Spinning Chinaman with an eager Douglas ready to put me through some ticklish paces. And Stephanie was just drunk enough for Valerie to seduce her out of her clothes and into who knows what. Valerie was getting wet between her legs as they stepped into the large bedroom. It seemed that this time out both my wife and I were in a stew of trouble.

Stephanie went to the closet for her new sexy lingerie, and Val sprawled out on the bed, pulling her dress up and showing lots of bare leg. Stephanie returned with several sets of skimpy, gauzy little things that were almost smaller than the hangers they were on. "Here they are. They aren't much, but in this case, Timmy had rather I pay more for less! Ha, ha."

As Steph spread the garments out on the bed, she noticed Val's bare legs and feet on the bed. "Val, you do have great legs. Timmy's right, you have the legs of a dancer...long, slender but muscular. You just have great legs." With that, Val took one leg and posed it up in the air with a ballerina toe point. She moved it round in small circles and then actually reached over with her bare foot and rubbed Steph's cheek. Stephanie was actually just drunk enough to not respond negatively to Val's action. Instead, she succumbed to the sexy soft foot rubbing her cheek, and just closed her eyes and smiled.

Val smiled to at Steph's reaction and Val jumped up from the bed and shucked her blouse and then her skirt. So, then as she moved behind Steph, she was down to just her bra and panties. Steph was still standing there with her eyes closed. Val pressed her nearly nude body up against Steph's back and reached around to her friend's blouse buttons. Val nuzzled Steph's neck and ear as she made quick work undoing those buttons. "Well, if we're going to try on your VS lingerie, we need to get rid of this blouse! Val whispered in Stephanie's ear. In her tipsy state, Steph was enjoying the attention like she was being pampered.

Next, Val unbuttoned and unzipped Steph's skirt and just let it drop to her feet. "We also need to get you out of this skirt...there!" Both women were now in just bra and panties. Except Steph was still sporting her high-heels. "You know, these VS clothes are so sheer and sexy...we'll have to remove these." And Val, having already removed her bra, held it out in front of Steph and let it drop to the floor. Stephanie just sort of blinked as Val reached back and undid the fastener on Steph's bra and pushed the straps forward off her shoulders. As Val did this, still nuzzling Steph's neck, she peered down at the two creamy spheres that were now no longer concealed in that Maiden form. Val let Steph's bra join her own on the floor, bringing her hands back to Steph's chest and her warm soft breasts, with the dark brownish areoles, and the nipples that were hardening by the second. Vals own nipples were stiffening up and pressing into Steph's back like two large pencil erasers...

Stephanie seemed to be in a trance because of the alcohol and attention, and was just enjoying what she was feeling as Valerie worked on her from the rear. "Oh Steph, you are so beautiful...so sexy...so desirable!" Val whispered into Step's ear. Then letting her hands slide down Steph's belly, Val snagged the elastic of the panties with her thumbs and began lowering them to the floor, squatting as she went. She also helped Stephanie out of her shoes while at the floor level. Now, Stephanie was standing there with her blouse skirt bra and panties pooled at her feet. As she stood back up, Val quickly eliminated her own panties, leaving them both... completely naked.

Val then moved around in front of Stephanie's luscious naked body. Now standing face to face, breasts to breast and belly to belly, Val looked deeply in the dilated eyes of her good friend. Val reached around Steph and pulled, pressing their bodies together...their breasts mashing into each other. Then, with open mouth, Val kissed Stephanie and was pleasantly surprised to feel Steph reciprocate. Val was lucky. Stephanie was just following her lustful feelings. Soon, they were moaning and groaning and grinding their mouths, breasts, bellies and their pussies together. This is what Valerie was hoping for and again, Stephanie was just giving in to her body's lustful feelings, even if this was her best friend, another woman.

After a few lustful moments of hugging and moaning and kissing, Valerie slowly pulled Stephanie down on the bed and they kissed and hugged some more and then began to grope each other like two long lost lovers. Valerie's cunt had been dripping earlier, but now they were both getting sloppy with lust. Valerie was in heaven. She had lusted after Stephanie ever since they had known each other. But Stephanie had been married and seemed to just ignore Val's previous little sexual hints. They were both really getting into this kissing and groping session. In fact it didn't take long, even without any kind of virginal penetration; they both came in buckets and squealed in the throes of that orgasm.

After cumming, Stephanie slumped back on the bed in exhaustion. "Val, what just happened? Did we just make love to each other?" Stephanie was exhausted, still tipsy, and filled with those after orgasm feelings. "Val, that was wonderful, but, I've never kissed a woman before...not like that. I've never hugged a woman before...not like that. And I've never made love...with a woman before...like that or any other way. Oh Val!" Steph moaned and closed her eyes.

But, Val had some other plans too. She was not through making love with and to Stephanie and, as Stephanie relaxed, Val slid up on top of her prone friend, but turned to face Stephanie's crotch and still steaming pussy while at the same time she pressed her own love canal toward Stephanie's face. Valerie then hooked Stephanie's thighs under her arms and pulled her legs and feet up into the air, pointing Steph's snatch at the ceiling. This not only completely exposed Stephanie's pussy, but also further back beyond to include her little brown button of an asshole. Stephanie was in a very sexually vulnerable position and was still incredibly sexually stimulated. Although she had been satisfied once, her pussy lips were still swollen and sensitive...just waiting further sexual contact.

Now, with Stephanie in this position, Valerie began to work her magic with her mouth and tongue on Stephanie's eager sensitive pussy. She also began to use her fingernails to stroke scrape the backs of Steph's thighs and even her ass cheeks and slipping ever closer to Stephanie's little brown button.

"Hee hee, he hee hee!" Stephanie giggled, "Val, he he he, that tickles. Oooo OH, he he he. Oh Val, he he he, that tickles." But it not only tickled, Val's tongue was turning up the heat in Stephanie's box again. "OH Val, OH Val, you're turning me on again, he he, OH Val!" Stephanie moaned and wiggled her hips with new lust and also trying to escape Valerie's fingernails. The girls had long forgotten the VS lingerie. There was just lust in their minds now.

As Valerie probed Stephanie with her educated tongue, she also pressed her own sex back toward Stephanie's face. Stephanie, even after one great orgasm, was building toward another because of Val's tongue. Now, her olfactory senses were adding to her sexual stimulation and Val's pungent aroma was wafting off her wet pussy lips and teasing Stephanie's nostrils.

Then Valerie noticed something at the foot of the bed. Could it be? She stopped her sexual stimulation of her friend and turning and rising up enough to look at the headboard. Yes, they are there too. Thinking to herself, "Stephanie, you devil. You've been tying Timmy up to this bed and just what have you been doing? You little devil you."

So, Valerie returned to licking and probing Stephanie's pussy and bringing her to a peak. Then once Stephanie's breathing and moaning indicated her orgasm was mounting, Val lets Stephanie's feet down so her legs were straight out. Then she stretched herself and grasped what turned out to be Velcro straps tied at the corners. This made securing Stephanie's ankles to the bed easy. Stephanie was oblivious. Once Val had done this, she turned once again to be face to face with Stephanie. She pushed Stephanie's arms up and out and taking the other Velcro straps, she secured Stephanie's wrists. Then she returned to kissing Stephanie and massaging her ample titties.

"Oh Val," Stephanie mumbled as she tugged on her arms and started looking back to where her wrists were now strapped to the bed. Even though she was drunk and about to have her second orgasm, she realized that her arms had been strapped to either corner of the bed. "Val! My arms. What have you done?"

"Stephanie darling, I just used those things that I found here on your bed. Now I know you well enough to know that Timmy doesn't tie you down to this bed. So, you must use those straps to tie poor ticklish Timmy down. And just what is it that you do to poor Timmy when you have him tied down like you are.

Stephanie was frantic! She was actually at the doorstep of a second orgasm. Her pussy was dripping once more and begging to be touched. Especially since she came last time with no virginal contact...just pure lust. But now, she found that Valerie had discovered the Velcro straps that she normally used on Timmy when she would lay him out spread-eagle and tickle his poor body till he's sweating and about to shoot his load. Timmy gets sooo sexy when he's tickled. "Valerie! Honey! Just what are you doing?" Stephanie asked, still panting from her sexual excitement, her hips grinding trying to find something to make contact with her pussy. Even through her tipsy haze, Stephanie knew that she just may be in trouble. Valerie had an evil look in her eye.

"Weeell, Steph, I found these Velcro restraints here in your and Timmy's bed. Now I would bet a year's commissions that Timmy doesn't use these on you...now does he...hmmm!" Valerie was seductively teasing Stephanie. "But, I bet Timmy would give me a year's commission to have you right where I have you...now wouldn't he...hmmm!"

"Val, let me out of these things!" Stephanie demanded. But, Valerie just took her index finger and began to massage Stephanie's outer pussy lips that were swollen and wet.

"OH, GOD! VAL FUCK, VAL, VAL. STICK IT IN ME! VAL, VAL OH GAD! OH SHIT MAKE ME...DAMN" Stephanie yelled in pure lust as Valerie kept teasing her pussy.

"Honey, Honey! I know you want to cum. But, we're going to have some fun first." And Valerie again assumed the 69 position. But, this time she made sure that her own pussy was pressed into Stephanie's face. And as Valerie began to tongue Stephanie's sex craving pussy, she was rewarded as Stephanie also began tonguing her pussy back. Knowing that Stephanie was now crazy with lust, Valerie timed her tongue dance. And every time Valerie paused, Stephanie picked up her tonguing pace in hopes that Valerie would reciprocate enough to bring her off. This went on for ten maybe fifteen minutes, with Valerie keeping Stephanie right on the edge, while enjoying Stephanie's energetic tonguing.

Until, Valerie came for the second time that evening, raring back and squealing at the ceiling and spilling her juices in Stephanie's face.

"NO! NO!" Stephanie screamed when Valerie left her pussy without a tongue. "Val, you can't stop! No! Come on Val...don't stop now. Gad Val...make me cum." Stephanie was delirious with lust. Any drunkenness that remained had now been supplanted by pure unadulterated lust and a desire to be brought to orgasm. Stephanie was thrashing her head about, although she was pretty well confined between Valerie's thighs. And she was yelling and screaming right into Valerie's pussy. Valerie simply squeezed her thighs against Stephanie's head as the last quakes of her orgasm passed through her body.

Lowering herself back down onto Stephanie's spread-eagle body Valerie relaxed for a moment, even though she still had a sex crazed and starved woman yelling and shaking and making all kinds of noises down between her legs. And she knew that Stephanie's antics down there would soon get her stimulated and sexed up again. Oh what fun.

"Now Stephanie Honey! That was so good! You really made me cum... goood that last time. And you know what?" There was nothing intelligible to be heard from Stephanie. Whatever she was saying or yelling was muffled by Valerie's thighs. "I think I know a way to get you to bring me off again, Honey." Valerie hummed seductively as she began to stretch and extend her hands out Stephanie's legs toward her bare feet, strapped to the corners of the bed.

And Valerie's fingernails started their tickling before they ever got to Stephanie's feet. And she began to hear Stephanie's muffled cries, "MO, MO, SNOFF NON'T MO, MO MOT MY FEEETH" Once Valerie began to tickle Stephanie's feet in earnest, Stephanie began to bounce and vibrate as she laughed. And all the laughing was right into Valerie's pussy and along with the bouncing and vibrating, Valerie was soon back to the brink of cumming again...for the third time that evening. The more Valerie tickled Stephanie's feet, the more Stephanie laughed and vibrated and the more that stimulated Valerie's pussy, the closer she got to cumming again. And Valerie kept tickling Stephanie's feet until she DID cum for the third time.

Now, Valerie had cum to orgasm three times and poor Stephanie had only cum once, and her pussy was craving attention...sort of like the itch you can't scratch. Valerie quit tickling Stephanie, rolled off the tethered young lady and rested for a moment. Stephanie was still hot as a branding iron, but she was panting and trying to recover from the tickling. The more she recovered from the tickling the more her lust for an orgasm moved to the forefront. Valerie got a damp cloth from the bathroom and washed her own juices from Stephanie's face. Stephanie was appreciative for the face cleaning and for the end to the tickling. But, she was still burning for an orgasm...her hips just would not stay still.

"Val Honey, I'm so hot. Oh shit, you've got me burning. I've got to cum. I need Timmy. Can you get him for me...I need him." Stephanie said with desperation.

"Darling Stephanie, Timmy is not available right now. Remember? He's showing Douglas the Spinning Chinaman. And, if I know Douglas...he had lots of questions that Timmy will not be able to answer. Plus I bet he's found out just how ticklish Timmy is. And, Douglas just loves to tickle...especially guys!" Valerie stated with a chuckle. "So, Steph dear, it's just you and me." Valerie dropped the washcloth and skimmed her hand and fingernails down over Stephanie's breasts, paying special attention to her still hard nipples.

Stephanie moaned, "Oh Val, I need Timmy...I need a dick...I need something in me...and I need it now!"

Valerie's hand moved lower playing slightly with Stephanie's ribs and the soft swell of her belly...circling her navel, and drawing giggles from her sex starved prisoner. Then she moved her hand lower continuing toward its sexual target. Valerie let her finger play in Stephanie's pubic hairs. Stephanie began to pump her hips up and down, searching for contact...penetration. She was craving to be fucked. Then Valerie removed her hand.

"NO, VAL! NO, COME ON VAL, DON'T STOP NOW!" Stephanie was going crazy.

"Look what I found in your dresser drawer Honey!" Valerie sang as she held up a big stiff goose feather that Stephanie had used on Timmy, many times.

Stephanie's eyes grew large with the realization that she was about to feel exactly what she had been doing to me these many years. She's so sexy and persuasive and I am so ticklish that I've never gotten the upper hand and she has always enjoyed the devilish delight of being the tickler and teaser. But, Valerie had managed to stimulate all of Stephanie's sexual buttons to the point that Stephanie was totally helpless and totally vulnerable to whatever Valerie wanted to do. And Valerie took that feather and toyed with Stephanie's already rigid nipples that were really standing out from her areoles. Valerie played with the nipples and then began trailing the feather lower toward Stephanie's belly. Stephanie was by then out of her mind with lust, but tickling...

"NO, VAL! YOU CAN'T BE SERIOUS, DON'T YOU DARE TICKLE ME WITH THAT FEATHER. COME ON NOW! Stephanie pleaded as loudly as she could. "TIMMY, TIMMY...WHERE THE FUCK ARE YOU...EEEEEEE HA HA HA HA HA HE HE EEEEEEE HA HA HA HA HA! Stephanie went off in a stream of laughter and Valerie spun the feather in her navel and ran it up her ribs and in and out of her armpits. "TIMMY HA HA HA EEEEEE HE HE HE TIMMY TIMMY!"

Valerie giggled and Stephanie's reaction, "Steph Honey, I do not believe that Timmy can hear you. If you notice, he's not come looking for us. I'd say that Douglas has Mr. Timmy occupied on your Spinning Chinaman. And if I know Douglas, he'll manage to strip and tickle him for as long as you and I are occupied. So, you just might as well forget Timmy coming to your rescue. Now, how ticklish are those pretty feet of yours?" Valerie continued to tickle torture Stephanie well into the evening to include using that feather on her swollen and sexy starved vagina. Stephanie was experiencing first hand the pleasure and agony of being teased and tickled by an artist.

Eventually, Valerie did get Stephanie off. So, she didn't just make her suffer totally. And Valerie fingered herself to a number of orgasms while tickling and teasing her friend. Finally, both girls seemed to be at the point of exhaustion. Valerie released Stephanie from her Velcro restrains and the girls both collapsed on the bed.

In about ten minutes, Stephanie recovered first. Apparently Valerie had fallen into a post sex slumber. Well, the dominant in Stephanie took over and she rolled over climbing in between Valerie's dancer-like legs. She pushed them apart and began licking Valerie's pussy lips and teasing and probing them with her tongue. Valerie began to moan and wiggle but she didn't seem to come fully awake. Then Stephanie moved Valerie to the center of the bed kissing her deeply and pushing her arms up over her head and out toward the corners, until she could secure Valerie's wrists in those same Velcro straps. Now, Valerie looked at Stephanie incredulously, "Honey, what do you think you're doing?"

"Oh! I'm just making sure that you can't stop me from kissing and licking your snatch!" Stephanie giggled and she climbed back between Valerie's dancer-like legs...resuming her tongue action. Now, Valerie had gotten off a number of times this evening, but Stephanie quickly brought her back to sexual peak once more. But now, Stephanie's goal was to just keep Valerie steaming on the edge of orgasm but not let her over the edge.

Soon, Valerie was begging Stephanie to bring her off, "Stef, come on now. Let's get on with this...I need for you to make me cum...NOW STEF! DO YOU HEAR ME! I-I NEED TO CU-CUM NO-NOW! OH FUCK YOU MAKE ME CUM!

Stephanie chuckled at Valerie's pleadings and determined that Valerie was ripe for the next step. So, Stephanie began licking Valerie's pussy in earnest. But, at the same time she began to elevate and push those great dancer legs up and back toward the headboard. Valerie was too centered on the ecstasy pouring from her pussy to be concerned with anything else. Stephanie kept working on Valerie, bringing her to the tingling edge of yet another orgasm...but Stephanie just kept Valerie there at the edge. Then Stephanie pushed Valerie's legs farther up over her head bending her in two, as if to get at her better...Valerie, lost in her lust submitted. But, Stephanie had another set of Velcro straps that Valerie hadn't seen earlier. With this second set of straps, Stephanie secured Valerie's ankles to the headboard near her wrists. Now Valerie was bent double with both her ankles and wrists strapped near each other at the headboard. Bent double and widely exposing both her pussy and her little brown asshole. This really left Valerie vulnerable and Stephanie began to return two fold all the pleasurable agony that she had received from the soon to be screaming and laughing Valerie.

So, with Valerie secured to the headboard, Stephanie relaxed back on the bed and retrieved her now warm wine and sipped as Valerie became aware of her predicament and all of her sexy plans and how they had now backfired.

"Stephanie Honey," Valerie tried to sweet-talk Stephanie, "Uh, this is not really a comfortable position, Honey. Can you at least let my legs down?"

"Oh, no!" Stephanie scolded. "Then I would not have a good access to your beautiful sex." And, Stephanie massaged Valerie's pussy lips till she was really wet and moaning again. Then Stephanie took a couple of big stiff feathers and worked on Valerie's nipples. They were already stiff, but they really got hard with the feather action and Valerie started screaming with laughter. The dildo was still buzzing in her dripping pussy. But, now she had other sensations.

"EEEEEE, STEPH, HE HE HEEE HE HE, STEPH PLEASE, HA HA AAAAH HA HA, STOP, HE HE HE DON'T TICKLE MY NIPPLES, HEE HEE HEE." Valerie squealed and laughed and carried on. But, Stephanie didn't stop with her nipples. She trailed those feathers to her armpits and literally danced them in those hollows. Then she moved the instruments of torment down Valerie's sides and belly and Valerie bucked. Then Stephanie started up the back of Valerie's exquisite dancer-like legs. Valerie's laughter tapered off until the feathers found the backs of her knees...and then tapered off again until Stephanie came to Valerie's pretty naked tootsies. Valerie could wiggle her feet and splay her toes, but she could not get away from the tickling feathers that Stephanie wielded. Stephanie tortured Valerie like this for a while, occasionally removing the vibrating dildo to use it to bring herself off.

Then Stephanie decided to give Valerie somewhat of a rest at least from the tickling. She turned up the vibrator and left Valerie tied doubled up to try and get herself off without squirting the dildo out.

"Val Dear, if you cause that dildo to squirt out of your honey pot, you'll just be left cum-less with nobody to play with. I'm going to check on Timmy." Stephanie announced as she slipped on her silk robe and tied the sash in a bow.

"Steph, please don't leave me. Please bring me off. Come on Steph!" Valerie pleaded, but Stephanie was quickly out the door and Valerie was left tied to the headboard with that slippery dildo vibrating in her pussy. She was horny as all hell and she could feel it slip like it would squirt out of her pussy, if she was not careful. And, that would leave her without satisfaction and she desperately needed that now.

Before Stephanie got to the living room, she could hear my squeals and laughter. She giggled as she imagined my plight. She and Valerie had left poor me, strapped in the Spinning Chinaman with Valerie's gay friend, Douglas. Obviously Douglas had taken the question game beyond just spinning for a wrong answer, and had added tickling as part of the penalty for a wrong answer.

But, Stephanie was shocked, but totally amused at the same time when she stepped into the living room that was filled with my laughter and squeals. There was her hubby, naked as the day he was born with Douglas tickling him all over with big stiff feathers. Because Stephanie enjoyed tickling me so danged much, she kept feathers in almost every room of the house. So, that if a tickling situation arose, she could grab a feather and go to work on her ticklish husband. Obviously Douglas had found some and was using them with abandon on my naked body. But, not only was I naked, Douglas was equally disrobed. Neither one of us had a stitch of clothing on...nothing, nil, nada! I wasn't even wearing my Christopher Trevor trademark black socks this time out. AND, Douglas and I were both sporting huge enflamed erections that were just dripping, ready to explode into orgasm. My dick would bounce as I squealed and laughed. Douglas's equally impressive root bounded and bobbed as he danced around tickling me. We were a sight and Stephanie almost hated to interrupt.

"Well, well, well!" Stephanie chided as she moved into the living room. Both of us guy's heads snapped toward her...Douglas looking like he'd been caught with his hand in the cookie jar...and me with the look of thanks for the arriving cavalry.

"OOOOh hoo hoo hoo ooo! Steph Honey! Thank goodness you're here, he he he. He's tickling me to death. Get me out of this thing!" I whined and caught my breath as my laughter slowly subsided. Douglas just stood there, a feather in each hand, a red enflamed dick protruding from his crotch, and a deer in the headlights look on his face.

"Oh Timmy Darling, what have you gotten yourself into now?" I left you fully clothed just a couple of hours ago and you were showing Douglas how the Spinning Chinaman works. Now, look at you...look at both of you. You're naked and being tickled by Douglas, and he's just as naked as you are. How did this happen?" Stephanie scolded...but she trying not to break out laughing.

"Steph Honey, please get me down from here. I can't take any more." I wailed and Douglas stammered.

"Well Steph, we started playing the Chinaman game like Timmy explained it to me. You know? I ask a question and he gets spun for a wrong answer. Well, I got bored with that and just changed the rules a bit. I told Timmy he could either be spun or tickled, but he had to tell me to do the opposite. Plus if he told me not to tickle him, or to stop tickling him then it would add a minute to his tickling." Douglas explained.

"Very interesting. But, how did you both get naked?" she inquired.

"Oh, another wrinkle to the game was if Timmy laughed when tickled...he would lose a piece of clothing. Well, then when he didn't have any more clothes to lose, I helped out...I removed a piece of my clothing when he laughed. So, eventually we were both naked. That's when I just started tickling him...pretty much non-stop." Douglas just stood there as he finished his explanation.

Stephanie smiled at Douglas and stroked his dick that was still bouncing in front of his crotch. "And you have a really nice package, Douglas. It's sort of a shame that a woman doesn't have the pleasure of the use of it."

Douglas moaned at Stephanie's touch. He was already so sexually excited, it didn't matter who touched his dick...it would cause him to moan. "Oh, Valerie will coax me into letting her ride me sometimes. And she is a friend, so I accommodate her."

"Ah, so even though you prefer guys, you will roll in the hay with Valerie?"

"Yeah!" Douglas admitted.

"Steph! What in the hell are you talking about?" I roared at her conversation and seeing her touch Douglas so intimately...another man.

But Stephanie just ignored me. "Would you like to join Timmy up on the Chinaman? I can put you up there with your naked backs together and set you up where you can tickle and tease each other...how does that sound?" She just giggled at this impromptu plan.

"Steph! What! What in the hell are you talking about? Get me down from here right now!" I demanded.

Still ignoring my demands, Stephanie continued talking to the naked Douglas, who was becoming more interested in what she was saying. "I have this Tense device that electrically tickles, massages and stimulates the muscles. And I use it to relax but I also use it to automatically tickle Timmy sometimes. Even when we are out and away from home. I can attach the base unit here to the waist strap on the Chinaman and then put one of the leads under his arm and these two on his nipples...that will drive him crazy...here's the coup-de-gras, I put the last lead right here behind his balls. Now, once you're up in the Chinaman, I'll let you have the Tense control...and you can tickle and tease Timmy to your dick's content."

"STEPHANIE, WHAT ARE YOU DOING? YOU CAN'T DO THIS! YOU'RE MY WIFE. YOU CAN'T..."

Stephanie cut me off, "Now Douglas, I also have a double headed vibrating dildo that we can connect you two boys with...how does that sound?" she giggled.

Douglas's eyes lit up as he listened to the gorgeous woman, who happened to be my wife, basically deliver her sexy husband to him for more sex play. "Why...that would be great...YES!" Douglas was really getting excited and his dick actually leaped.

So Stephanie got the double headed vibrating dildo and lubricated one end and slid it up my ass. Of course I protested mightily...but to no avail. Then she helped Douglas up onto the Chinaman, lubed the other end of the dildo and Douglas accepted it up his ass, a lot more readily and happily than I did. Now we two naked guys were both strapped into the Spinning Chinaman back to back. Our naked flesh pressed together from head to heel, but we were connected by the dildo at our asses.

"Now Timmy, to be fair, I'm going to give you the remote control to the vibrating dildo. This way you can stimulate Douglas's ass and try to distract him from pressing the Tense activation button that will tickle the shit out of you. The catch is that, since the dildo is double headed, you'll get the same dose of vibrations that you give Douglas...doesn't that sound like fun." Stephanie continued to giggle at my naked predicament. If I didn't activate the dildo, Douglas would be free to activate the Tense device that would tickle and tease me under my arm, on my nipples and behind my danged balls. But, if I activated the dildo, in order to vibrate Douglas' ass and distract him from pressing the Tense activator...I would, myself get an ass vibration. Dang, I would be tickled if I didn't and vibrated if I did.

Now we two naked guys were strapped into the Spinning Chinaman, ass to ass with our engorged dicks pointing in opposite directions. I squealed and laughed as Douglas pressed the Tense activator. Then I, in an attempt to draw Douglas's attention away from the Tense button, activated the double headed vibrating dildo and both of us groaned as the vibrations took hold. Douglas did release the Tense button as he felt the dildo buzz him right up through his prostate. But, I quickly experienced the same feelings and released the dildo activator button. Once, the vibrations stopped, Douglas again pressed the Tense button, sending me off on another laughing binge. Stephanie watched us go back and forth, with me obviously getting the worst of this arrangement. But, it was major amusing. Our dicks were dripping with pre-cum in a matter of minutes. At this rate, we would tease each other and not be able to get off... what a predicament we were in.

Just to add to our pleasure...ha ha...Stephanie took and spun the Chinaman like she was playing WHEEL OF FORTURE. As we spun and teased and tickled each other, Stephanie giggled and went back to see about Valerie. What a double date this turned out to be. As she left the room with the Chinaman spinning its riders, Stephanie could hear my high pitched squeals and laughter as Douglas pressed the activator on the Tense remote. She could also hear the pleasure groans from Douglas as I was activating the double headed dildo, vibrating both of our asses and prostates and driving both of us toward orgasm. But, then in his excitement Douglas released the activator button on the Tense, which stopped my tickling. And in turn I stopped the vibrator in relief of the stopped tickling. Stephanie laughed at our plight as she glanced back at the spinning naked bodies in our living room. What's funny is that the way we were spinning, our protruding dicks looked like an axle on which they were turning. And the noises we were making...how funny...how sexy.

Leaving us boys to our own self torture, Stephanie returned to our bedroom to check on Valerie's status. When she stepped into the room, she found Valerie sweating and humping the air with her ass, being teased by the vibrating dildo riding in her pussy. But, trying her best not to dislodge it and lose contact with the potential ecstasy it could bring her. But, she was showing the frustration of trying to cum but yet just hovering at the brink and not being able to take herself over. Her hair was now ringing wet. Stephanie just smiled at herself, thinking, "I have just outdone myself. I have three people driving themselves crazy with lust but just not quite able to finish the job. How amusing."

So, Stephanie shed her silk robe and rejoined Valerie on the bed. Valerie barely acknowledged Stephanie's return through her lust crazed eyes. Stephanie smiled and twisted the control on the vibrator to MAX and Valerie began to hump in earnest. But, Stephanie picked up the discarded feathers and began to bring back Valerie's laughter...big time. "Oh Valerie...You are one ticklish little girl! I think it's going to be a very, very long evening here..."

# ELI MEETS DR. TICK LEE

## Written by: Christopher Trevor

*Story dedicated to: my good buddy Daryll for input and incentive...*

"Ohhhhhhrrrrrrr God Coach, it's broken, it's fuckin' broken! *I just know it's broken*! Fuck, but it feels awful!" Eli grunted in pain, referring to his left foot that he had just taken a mean twist on out on the University of Mississippi College football field.

"Take it easy Eli, take it easy, we'll find out soon enough," the coach said as he held Eli's big sneaker feet together at the calves under his muscular arms as he and two of the other college football players carried the injured young man into the team's locker room. "From where I was standing on the field I could see the way you landed on that foot and I'm pretty sure that all you did was twist your ankle..."

Alex and Dennis, two of the other football players were supporting Eli's upper body, Eli's muscular and brawny arms wrapped around their middle backs as they hauled him along.

"Th-then why the hell does it feel like its broken Coach?" Eli asked breathlessly as they headed for a massage table in the locker room.

Eli was doing all he could not to cry, the pain was that awful.

"Eli, have you ever had a broken foot before?" the coach asked his star player as he and the other two player's carried him.

"Nah, no, I never did Coach," Eli replied.

"Then you don't know how it would feel if it's broken," the coach said as they reached the massage table, trying to sound as reassuring for the young man as for himself as possible.

The coach knew that without Eli out there on the field his team would not stand a chance of winning anymore games this season; and he intended to be in the college championships this year. Eli's foot could not be broken the coach prayed, *it just couldn't be*!

"Trust me son, sometimes a mean twist can feel like a broken foot, the pain can be that intense..." the coach went on reassuringly as he and the other two footballers hefted Eli over the massage table. "Okay guys, lift him a tad higher and then set him down gently on the table here..."

Alex and Dennis took a deep breath each and lifted Eli's muscular body over the table and then gently set him down on his back as the coach laid his feet down as well.

"Damn Eli, you sure are one heavy fucker," Alex said, patting his football buddy on the head.

"It's all that equipment he's still got on," the coach said, beginning to unlace Eli's high-top sneakers as he spoke. "Get those shoulder pads and knee pads off him so he'll be more comfortable. Eli, I'm going to take your sneakers and socks off you so I can check to see if there's any swelling on your left foot. That's the one you twisted, correct?"

"C-correct Coach," Eli said as his shoulder pads were removed and he laid his head back more comfortably upon the padded table.

"Okay, what I'll need to see is if your left foot is swollen as compared to your right foot," the coach explained as Alex and Dennis hurriedly got Eli's kneepads off him.

"Yeah, and if it is that mean's it's broken, right?" Eli asked, clenching his teeth as he gripped the sides of the table he was on, the bowling ball sized biceps in his arms protruding real paramount just under the short sleeves of his navy blue and white football Jersey.

"Not necessarily son, as I already said, it could just mean that you twisted the ankle real intensely," the coach said and then gripped Eli's left sneaker after getting the laces undone. "Okay Eli, this might hurt a bit as I take the sneaker off you so just try to deal with it okay?"

"Y-yeah, sure Coach," Eli said and gripped the sides of the table tighter.

"Hey Eli, you want a bullet to bight on?" Dennis asked his buddy, sounding snide and leaning down over him in an almost lecherous way.

"F-fuck you Dennis," Eli grunted with a real shit eating grin on his face, trying to put up a manly front as the pain tore through him.

Eli always had a feeling somewhere deep inside him that Dennis wanted more than just to be football buddies with him. Eli couldn't have cared less about Dennis's feelings; he was a good football player like him and because of him and Dennis their college football team was in first place the last two years. If Dennis harbored secret feelings for him Eli could not have given it a second thought... Football was what was important, and at this moment, his left foot not being broken was even more important...

"OWWWWWRRR!" Eli suddenly grunted loud and in pain as his sneaker was slipped off his left injured foot.

"Okay son, it's off, that should be the worst of it for the moment," the coach said and began unlacing Eli's other sneaker.

Eli, Alex and Dennis watched as the coach got the injured player's other sneaker off him...

"Hmm, I'll have to get your sweat socks off you too Eli," the coach said, grabbing the tops of Eli's pushed down white sweat socks with his fingers and thumbs. "No way can I tell if your left foot is swollen with your thick socks on you..."

"Yeah, yeah, whatever it takes Coach..." Eli said, hefting himself up on his elbows to get a look at his left foot once it would be revealed.

As the coach whipped Eli's socks off him Eli felt Dennis's hand squeezing his shoulder in a reassuring way. Once his socks were off his feet though Eli felt Dennis's grip on his shoulder tighten.

"W-well, what do you think Coach?" Eli asked his mentor.

"I haven't looked closely enough yet Eli, relax," the coach said and then gently took Eli's bare feet in his fingers and thumbs and leaned down close to inspect them.

"Hey Coach, if I know Eli his feet are probably real rank right about now," Dennis quipped, holding tighter yet to Eli's shoulder.

"F-fuck you again Dennis," Eli said, once again with that shit eating grin on his face.

"Doesn't matter how his feet smell Dennis," the coach said, holding his player's big bare feet gently, almost lovingly in his hands. "What matters is that our star player here *not* has a broken ankle..."

Eli, Dennis and Alex all watched as the coach inspected the injured player's feet. Eli had to wonder why his coach did seem to be taking deep breaths as he leaned over his big bare feet... Eli also knew that there was some truth to what Dennis had just stated, about how his feet would be pretty damned rank by now. Eli's feet always stunk real high after a long game out on the field... His roommate in the dorm always complained about how Eli's feet smelled so bad after he took his sneakers and socks off...

"Wh-what do you think Coach?" Eli asked again.

"Well, there definitely is some swelling," the coach replied as he trailed his fingers slowly along Eli's ankles. "I'm not going to lie to you. But I really don't think it's broken...maybe just a slight sprain or a hairline fracture..."

"H-how can you be sure?" Eli asked.

"I can't," the coach replied. "A doctor will have to make that determination. We better have you sent for x-rays post haste. I'll find someone who can drive you to the medical lab on campus. Is your girlfriend here watching the game today? Maybe she can drive you over to the lab."

"N-no, she had class today Coach," Eli moaned as the coach held his ankles, his fingers gently caressing the football star's deep and shapely arches. "She couldn't make the game..."

"I can take him Coach," Dennis piped up, sounding almost honored to do the task. "I have my car out in the field parking lot as it is. Plus someone will have to carry poor Eli here from the car and into the doctor's office at the lab. I doubt his girlfriend can do that, seeing as they don't have stretchers at the lab."

"Okay Dennis, change up and get our golden boy here over to the lab," the coach said, still caressing and gently squeezing Eli's feet. "Alex, you get back out on the field. I'll be there in a few minutes..."

"Yes Sir Coach!" Alex and Dennis said and went their separate ways, Alex back out on the field and Dennis over to his locker to get changed quickly out of his football uniform.

"I'll store your shoulder pads and knee pads in my locker Eli," the coach said, picking up Eli's equipment from the floor where it had been discarded. "I'm almost sure that the x-ray will show that it's only a slight hairline fracture. Very likely they'll wrap your foot in an ace bandage at the college medical lab and you'll have to stay off it for a few days."

"I sure as hell hope you're right Coach, *I sure as hell hope you're right...*" Eli said as the coach quickly stowed Eli's equipment in his nearby locker.

"I'll put your socks and sneakers in this bag for you son," the coach said, depositing Eli's footwear in a small duffel bag. "You'll more than likely need them after you're done getting that foot x-rayed."

"Thanks Coach," Eli said, taking the duffel from his coach. "Listen, I'm real sorry about all this..."

"Nothing to be sorry about, just come back with good news," the coach said and squeezed Eli's right foot affectionately. "And when I say come back with good news that includes being able to play in the next game..."

"Yes Sir Coach," Eli said and gave a thumb's up sign.

A few moments later Dennis returned clad now in jeans, sneakers and a pullover polo shirt.

"I'm all set Coach," Dennis said, looking at Eli somewhat hungrily. "I'll go and pull my car up to the back entranceway of the locker room, that way I won't have to carry Eli too far..."

"Yeah, he is a rather heavy muscle boy," the coach agreed and shook Dennis's hand. "Thanks for your help Dennis. Call me in my office as soon as the x-ray results are in..."

"Sure thing Coach," Dennis said and the coach left the two young men alone. "I'll be back in a jiffy Eli..."

"Thanks Dennis," Eli replied and lay back down on the table, his arms at his sides.

While Dennis went to get his car Eli tried his best to relax and endure the throbbing that was emanating from his ankle and up his leg...

"Ohhhhhh God, it's broken, *I just know it's fucking broken...*" Eli muttered miserably.

A short while later Dennis returned...

"Okay buddy, I got my car right out back," Dennis said. "The passenger door is open so I'll just put you right in. Sit up now and try to distribute your weight as evenly as possible for me okay?"

"Sure, yeah, okay," Eli said as Dennis inched his hands and upper arms under Eli's knees and under his back.

Dennis took a deep breath and lifted Eli into his muscular arms ala the style of a groom carrying his bride over the threshold.

"HUUUUFFFFF!" Dennis grunted as he hefted the star football player off the table. "Damn, I should have asked Alex and the coach to hang around so they could help me carry you to my car huh big guy?"

"Yeah or at least asked for a wheelchair or something," Eli said and wrapped an arm quickly around Dennis's back, trying to distribute his weight as much as possible.

"Good thing the coach makes us weight train five days a week huh buddy?" Dennis asked huffily and carried Eli toward the back door of the locker room. "Fuck man, but you really do weigh Eli."

"Y-yeah, I suppose so,' Eli replied and managed to catch the look in Dennis's eyes as he was lugged along.

Once outside Dennis gently deposited Eli in the passenger seat of his car, Eli holding the small duffel bag containing his socks and sneakers as Dennis closed the car door followed by the locker room door. As Dennis got comfortable in the driver's seat Eli rested his bare feet on the soft plush rug in front of him.

"Okay, I'll have you at Doctor Tick Lee's in no time buddy," Dennis said and started the car.

"Doctor Tick Lee?" Eli asked. "I never heard of a Doctor Tick Lee at the college medical lab..."

"That's because he's not at the college medical lab," Dennis explained. "He's at my doctor's office. He's an associate of my private doctor. He's also very new age in the healing of fractures..."

"Are you sure man?" Eli asked as Dennis drove off campus. "I mean, the coach said to take me to the college medical lab...and we're not even sure my ankle is fractured...I mean, my danged foot could be broken after all..."

"I know, I know, but trust me Eli, Doctor Tick Lee won't even have to bother with x-rays," Dennis went on, sounding totally positive about what he was talking about. "He'll know what to do just by looking at your injured foot..."

"If you say so man, I'm in too much pain to argue as it is..." Eli said and sat back in the seat, closing his eyes.

Had his eyes been open Eli would have seen the sinister smile playing across Dennis's lips as he drove...

A while later Dennis pulled up in front of a building that was set all by itself on a lonely looking road surrounded mostly by trees...

"Well, we're here..." Dennis said.

"Wh-where?" Eli asked as he opened his eyes and looked out the car window. "Gawd, I must have dozed off..."

"Still in pain?" Dennis asked.

"Y-yeah, but jeez man, what is this place?" Eli asked. "This sure as hell doesn't look like a doctor's office."

To Eli it looked like a desolate house set all by itself in an equally desolate looking area. If the college star football player didn't know better he would swear that Dennis had driven them to some remote place way out in the country. But that wasn't possible, seeing as it had felt like a short drive, hadn't it?

"Well, when we got to my doctor's I found out that Dr. Tick Lee was here at his private place," Dennis explained as he opened the driver's side door. "Once he heard that Miss University's star football player had been injured he agreed to see you in his private office. How does that sound buddy?"

Before Eli could reply Dennis was out of the car and sprinting around to the passenger side...

"I-I guess it sounds pretty flattering," Eli said as Dennis opened the passenger side door and made a cradle of his muscular arms for Eli. "Upsadaisy buddy boy..."

Before Eli allowed himself to be hoisted he looked deep into Dennis's eyes. The injured football player felt a slight stirring in his cock...

"Y-you uh, you don't have to carry me Dennis," Eli said. "Just let me hold onto your shoulder and I'll hop along on my good foot..." Eli said.

"Suit yourself bud," Dennis said as Eli climbed out of the car.

As the star football player went to stand up he grimaced miserably in pain as he accidentally set his injured foot down on the ground...

"AAAARRRHHHH jeez, fucking fuck!" Eli ranted and Dennis quickly scooped his good buddy up off the ground.

"I get the feeling that Dr. Tick Lee is going to see you right away buddy..." Dennis said as he lugged the heavy load of Eli to the front door of the strange looking building.

Eli looked around and felt a strange feeling of foreboding engulf him...

He held tight to the small duffel bag as he was carried...

"It's funny you know, how when a certain part of our body is injured we tend to favor it?" Dennis asked Eli.

"Wh-what do you mean?" Eli asked as he bounced in Dennis's arms.

"Well, the way you put your weight down on your injured foot just now instead of on your right one," Dennis pointed out. "Just something to wonder about...that's all..."

"Yeah, I see what you mean..." Eli agreed as they reached the door.

"Hey bud, would you mind reaching out and ringing the bell?" Dennis huffed. "My hands are kind of full, as you can plainly see...hardy har, har..."

"Hardy fucking har *and* har," Eli replied and did as he had been asked.

The door was opened by a very tall and very handsome Asian man dressed in a doctor's white coat over a shirt and tie. He had silky black wavy hair and dark slanted eyes. His eyes were somehow piercing Eli thought as he quickly took in the sight before him.

"Well, hello there, and you must be Eli," the doctor said in a half English half Asian sounding accent. "I am Doctor Tick Lee. And of course Dennis and I go back, way back, yes. Right this way please Dennis, right this way..."

Dennis, carrying Eli and sweating like crazy by then followed Dr. Tick Lee into an examination room, which looked more to the footballer like a mini operating room...

"Oh God man, I just know it's broken," Eli muttered miserably.

"Please, put him down on that table," Dr. Tick Lee said to Dennis and Dennis did as instructed.

Eli handed Dennis his duffel bag and stretched himself out atop the cushioned table.

"As I stated a few moments ago, I am Doctor Tick Lee," the Asian doctor said to Eli, again introducing himself, this time holding his hand out.

"G-good to meet you Dr. Tick Lee," Eli said and shook the doctor's hand, his huge football player hand dwarfing the doctor's hand in his.

Eli felt a shudder course through him for a moment as he felt the doctor's thin spidery fingers seem to caress the side of his hand as they shook.

"So, what seems to be the *exact* nature of the problem here?" the doctor asked Dennis as he let go of Eli's hand.

"Well Doctor Tick Lee, Eli here injured his left foot playing in today's college football game," Dennis explained as Eli squirmed atop the table, the pain in his ankle again shooting straight up his muscular leg.

"It's broken Doc, I know it is," Eli said through clenched teeth.

"Well now, I think perhaps I should be the judge of that don't you think?" the doctor asked with a grin, still standing at Eli's side. "Did anyone at the college look at it?"

"M-my coach, he thinks it's just a hairline fracture..." Eli said.

"Okay, lets get the young man secured to the table and then I'll need some information on him and then we'll get started examining that foot, yes?" Doctor Tick Lee asked and quickly reached under the table and produced two leather straps that were attached to the bottom portion of the table.

The doctor and Dennis worked quickly and efficiently in getting Eli's upper body strapped down tight.

"H-hey, what are you doing?" Eli asked.

"Nothing to be alarmed about young man, nothing to be alarmed about whatsoever, it's all for your own good," the doctor stated.

"M-my own good? But you're tyin' me to the table here..." Eli said, sounding just a tad above nervous.

"Yes, yes, I do not want you accidentally falling off table while I examine your hurt foot," the doctor said and proceeded to secure two straps over Eli's legs at the knees and just above his ankles.

"Oh jeez man," Eli said looking up into Dennis's fiendish looking eyes. "Somehow I get the feeling I've been had...buddy boy..."

"Nothing to worry about Eli, you're in good hands here," Dennis said and patted Eli on the cheek.

"Okay now, just some routine questions and then I'll start examining your friend's feet, er, his foot," Doctor Tick Lee said to Dennis.

"Sure thing Doc," Dennis said.

"How old is Eli?" the doctor asked.

"Uh, he's twenty," Dennis said.

"His height, weight?" the doctor went on.

"H-hey, I'm right here Doc," Eli said. "I can answer your questions for you..."

"No need Eli, you are in too much pain," the doctor said. "I will be with you very shortly...you just relax and lay there..."

Eli rolled his eyes in his head in disbelief and looked up at the ceiling. Strapped down the way he was all he could do was lay there, as the doctor had just instructed, but relax? GEEZ! When he heard the doctor ask Dennis, "What size are his feet?" Eli somehow knew then and there that he was in trouble... Just because his foot was hurt did not constitute a reason for the doctor knowing their size. Eli wiggled his toes nervously.

After all the necessary questions had been answered the doctor then turned his attention to the strapped down football player atop the table...

"So, lets see here Mr. Eli, brown hair, brown eyes, six feet four, give or take an inch, heh, heh, just a little joke there you understand," the doctor said sounding very fiendish and Eli could not help but notice that as the doctor said "give or take an inch" his eyes had been riveted on his big basket of a crotch. "Size eleven feet..."

It was at that moment that Eli realized he was still wearing his protective cup under his football uniform knickers.

"Yeah, that all sounds about right Doc," Eli said softly and wiggled the toes on his right foot. "Big ol' size eleven feet..."

"Okay then, let's take a look at that injured foot of yours shall we?" Doctor Tick Lee asked and stepped to the foot of the table.

"Uh Doctor Tick Lee, my uh, my friend Dennis here said that you would be able to determine if my foot was broken without even taking x-rays," Eli said, glancing up at Dennis as he stood at the table side. "Is, is that true?"

"Most true young Eli indeed is true," the Asian doctor said, holding up a long finger. "I can tell you already that foot is not broken."

"H-how can you tell me that already?" Eli asked.

"If foot was broken you would be howling in pain, as you Americans say," the doctor replied. "My guess is like your coach said, fracture, and slight maybe. But I will examine you to be sure..."

"Th-thanks Doc," Eli said as the doctor hunkered down by Eli's strapped down bare feet.

"Isn't he something?" Dennis whispered in Eli's ear, his tongue tip almost grazing Eli's earlobe as he spoke softly.

"Yeah, but what that something is I'm still trying to figure out..." Eli whispered in reply.

"Okay, is left foot that appears swollen, slight, but swollen," the doctor said and waved a hand in front of his face.

"Sorry Doc, my feet are always kind of rank after I play football for a few hours," Eli apologized as the doctor stood up straight.

Dennis smiled lecherously down at Eli, a knowing look on his face at the mention of Eli's rank scented bare feet...

"Not a problem young Eli," the doctor said, stepping over to a cabinet of drawers. "I will clean off your feet and then examine them, yes?"

"Uh, sure, but you'll only need to examine my left one," Eli said, correcting the doctor and looking upwards desperately at Dennis. "I mean, that's the one that's injured..."

"Of course, of course young Eli," the doctor said with a grin and then turned to open a drawer in the cabinet. "But both feet will need to be cleaned, yes?"

"Uh yes, I suppose so," Eli said, sounding unsure.

Actually the star footballer was unsure of this entire set-up.

Eli, with his head turned watched as the doctor took two long-stick cotton swabs from the drawer along with what looked like a bottle of alcohol or cleaner of some kind. While the doctor worked Dennis placed a hand on top of Eli's head and tousled his messy hair.

"Relax Eli, relax, Doctor Tick Lee is going to take good care of you," Dennis said and Eli looked up again at his buddy, this time with a hardy har, har look on his handsome face.

"Okay, this should do the *trick* I would think," Doctor Tick Lee said, holding up the items he had taken from the drawer.

He rolled a small table next to the one that Eli was strapped down to and set the long-stick cotton swabs and the bottle of alcohol or whatever the hell was in that bottle down on the table.

"Wh-what is that stuff Doc?" Eli asked as the doctor handed Dennis one of the long-stick cotton swabs.

"Just a soap and alcohol mixture young Eli, disinfectant for your feet if you would, soap to clean your feet and alcohol to kill any germs that might be there," the doctor said kindly and then looked at Dennis. "You won't mind helping me with Eli's feet will you Dennis?

"No Doctor Tick Lee, I won't mind at all," Dennis replied, sounding almost phony and somewhat theatrical.

Doctor Tick Lee and Dennis dipped their swabs into the bottle and swished them around in there.

"I-I guess it's cool," Eli said, sounding very unsure now.

After Dennis and the doctor had thoroughly soaked their cotton swabs in the mixture they stepped to the end of the table, the doctor wheeling the small table along with them.

"Okay young Eli, we will begin with your right foot," the doctor said and then he and Dennis trailed their swabs in up and down motions against the meaty bottom of Eli's foot.

"OOOOOOOOOO h-hey, th-that tickles, THAT TICKLES!" Eli sputtered. "Ha, ha, ha, ha, ha, ha, ha, ha, ha, ha, ha, ha!"

"Oh dear, are you a ticklish laddy?" Doctor Tick Lee asked his charge and he and Dennis smiled evilly at each other.

"Y-yes, I-I suppose I am, ha, ha, ha, ha, ha, ha, ha, ha, ha!" Eli laughed. "D-Dennis, you and the doc, s-say, you're ticklin' me here! Ha, ha, ha, ha, ha, ha, ha, ha, ha! DON'T! STOP! OH GAWD, that tickles! Ha, ha, ha, ha, ha, ha, ha, ha! OH PLEASE!"

Eli squirmed under the tight straps as the doctor moved the wet and cold swab over the fronts of his feet and then along his deep and shapely arches. At the same time Dennis continued tickle swabbing the bottom of Eli's foot, from the balls of it to the heel and back up again.

"HA, HA, HA, HA, HA, HA, HA, HA, HA, HA, HA, HA!" Eli laughed louder as the doctor and Dennis trailed their swabs over and over and over his right foot. "H-hey, what are you doing to me here Doc?"

"As stated, we are just cleaning up your feet for you young Eli," the doctor said gleefully and pressed his swab hard against Eli's heel and slid it meanly upwards as Dennis now tended to the front of Eli's foot with his swab.

"Yeah, didn't I tell you that Doctor Tick Lee would take good care of you Eli?" Dennis quipped.

"AAAAAAWWWWHAHAHA!" Eli blubbered. "S-sorry Doc, don't mean to laugh so loud here, ha, ha, ha, ha, ha, ha, ha, ha, b-but that sure as all hell tickles like the dick-dickens...HAHAHAHAHAHA!"

"I am also sorry Eli, but it is very funny, I mean, necessary, yes necessary, that all germs be removed from your feet," the doctor said with a reassuring smile as he and Dennis swabbed Eli's right foot more and more. "And being that your said feet are of the rather jumbo sized I would say that this may take some time."

"HARHARHARHARHARHARHAR!" Eli laughed, gripping the sides of the table, his massively muscular chest heaving under the tight straps.

Had the college star footballer not been strapped to the table he would have flown off it with what the doctor and Dennis did to him next.

"HAAAAAAAA!" Eli screamed in a high pitched tone of voice as the doctor and Dennis started sliding their moist swabs between his big thick toes. "OOOOOOOOOOOO G-gosh, b-but that's really ticklin' me now Doc! HAAAAA, HAAAAA, OOOOOOOO!"

Eli saw the look of ecstasy on his buddy Dennis's face as the guy held his pinky toe tight, yanked it to the side and swabbed in between there. All poor Eli could do was laugh and laugh...

While Dennis gripped Eli's pinky toe the doctor slid his swab between Eli's other toes at least five times each in both directions, going from his toe next to the pinky one to his big toe and then back again...he and Dennis really getting the star football player guffawing and screaming.

"HAR, HAR, HAR, HAR, HAR, HAR, HAR, HAR!" Eli laughed, gruntingly.

The doctor and Dennis dipped their swabs back in the bottle of the cleaner and once again began sliding them up and down the meaty bottom of Eli's right foot. If Eli didn't know better he would have sworn that the doctor and Dennis were actually taking turns in tickling his foot, both of them trying to see who could make Eli laugh the hardest.

"Wh-what are you doin' Doc?" Eli laughed. "HA, ha, ha, ha, ha, ha, ha, ha, ha, ha, ha! Y-you two cleaned the bottom of my f-foot already..."

"Each foot requires at least three to five good cleanings young Eli," the doctor said as he rubbed the swab over Eli's arch, trailing it along lasciviously as he did so, all the while Dennis was still swabbing the bottom of Eli's foot up and down and up and down, even making circular motions.

"Maybe even six to ten cleanings each Eli," Dennis quipped as he held Eli's toes tight and made circles on the bottoms of the footballer's meaty foot.

"HO, ho, ho, ho, ho, ho, ho, ho, ho, ho..." Eli laughed, his handsome head raised off the table and his teeth gnashing as he ho, ho, hoed and hoed some more.

After swabbing Eli's right foot five times each with their swabs the doctor and Dennis put the swabs down on the small table.

"You are sweating very profusely young Eli," the doctor said as he stepped over to a refrigerator and Dennis stood next to Eli, gently massaging his forehead. "Some water will do you well perhaps..."

"D-Dennis, what kind of nutty doctor have you brought me to?" Eli whispered up at his buddy as the doctor took a quart-sized bottle of mineral water from the refrigerator.

"Relax bud; he knows what he's doing..." Dennis whispered reassuringly.

"Knows what he's doing?" Eli whispered in a seething tone of voice. "You and he just tickled the fuck outa my danged foot..."

Eli quickly shut-up as the doctor approached the table with the bottle of mineral water...

Then, the doctor held Eli's head raised by the back as he held the quart sized bottle of strange tasting mineral water to the strapped down young man's lips. Despite the strange taste of the water Eli gratefully sipped the refreshing liquid down...

"Okay, now we will clean your left foot, that is the injured one, yes?" the doctor asked Eli after putting the bottle of mineral water down on the small table.

"Y-yes, that, that's the one that I twisted, so please be careful not to tickle me when you clean it Doc," Eli said, almost pleading, and then looked over at Dennis. "And that goes for you too buddy boy..."

"Well, let's try this then," the doctor said, stepped to the end of the table and grabbed Eli's left foot in both his hands.

"Wh-what are you doing Doc?" Eli asked in a panic as the doctor gripped his left foot tight.

Without replying and with Dennis looking on in wonderment the doctor gave Eli's left foot a twist in the right direction...

"ARRRRRRHHHHH!" Eli bantered and arched his muscular body under the tight and binding straps.

Then, the doctor, still holding tight to Eli's left foot twisted it in the left direction...

"AAAARRRRRHHHHH!" Eli roared again. "D-Dennis, what's he doin' to me man? He's really goin' to break my danged foot here..."

"How does it feel now young Eli?" the doctor asked his strapped down patient.

Eli looked up at Dennis and then down at his left foot and started wiggling his toes on it...

"Hey, HEY! Hey, it feels great!" Eli said triumphantly. "Y-you cured me Doc, holy Moses, you fixed my danged foot..."

"Well, I would not say that *exactly yet* young Eli," the doctor said, correcting the footballer. "All I actually did was twist the ankle back into place. The feeling of relief is only temporary you understand..."

"T-temporary?" Eli asked.

"Yes, so that if Dennis and I tickle you while cleansing your left foot it won't hurt as much if you squirm it around under the straps..." Doctor Tick Lee explained. "Not that I intend for us to tickle you mind you..."

"S-sure Doc, I'll just bet..." Eli said, looking up at Dennis with a determined look on his handsome face. "We'll talk once this is over...*buddy boy*..."

That said the doctor picked up the second long-stick swabs, handed one to Dennis and they both soaked them in the cleanser mixture.

"Oh dang it all..." Eli whispered as he watched the doctor and Dennis soak their swabs.

When the swabs were thoroughly socked Doctor Tick Lee and Dennis began trailing them up and down the bottom of Eli's left foot...

"Ha, ha, ha, ha, ha, ha, ha, ha, ha, ha, ha, ha, ha, ooooooooo, and here we go again!" Eli laughed.

"Oh my, it is a good thing then that I twisted your ankle back into place," the doctor said jovially as he and Dennis tickled Eli anew. "Once Dennis and I are done cleaning up your feet I am sure we will see just what that twist you took earlier today did to you..."

As the doctor spoke and cleaned/tickled Eli's foot Eli laughed louder and louder...

Poor Eli could not understand why he was strapped down and being tickled. He also could not understand the sudden stirring that was somehow engulfing his crotch area. He felt his cock start to stiffen under his protective cup in his football uniform knickers...

"HOOOOOOOOO GAWD!" the footballer panted as his manhood

started to swell in the protective cup that Eli had on.

"HARHARHARHARHAR! D-Doc, D-Dennis, p-please stop, please, please stop tickling me...HAHAHAHAHAHAHAHAHA!"

"I truly do not mean for what Dennis and I are doing to you to tickle you young Eli," the doctor said soothingly as he slid his swab along Eli's left arch while Dennis continued trailing his up and down the bottom of Eli's foot. "But I really do need your feet to be clean before I can begin any kind of a thorough examination...you understand I am sure..."

"Y-yeah sure, sure, I understand...HARHARHARHAR Oh holy fuck!" Eli screamed.

The doctor then began sliding his swab between the toes on Eli's left foot and making sawing motions between his toes, all the while Dennis trailed his swab continually up and down and up and down the bottom of Eli's foot.

"Are you sure you understand?" Eli heard the doctor say as he screamed his laughter once again as the spaces between his toes and the bottom of his foot were being tickled.

"HAW, HAW, HAW, HAW, HAW, HAW, l-like I said before," Eli guffawed crazily. S-somehow I think I've been, ha, ha, ha, ha, ha, ha, ha, ha, ha, ha, had! I've been had!"

Dennis looked worriedly at the doctor as he went on swabbing the bottom of Eli's foot in faster and faster up and down motions...

"I do not understand why you feel that way young Eli," the doctor said and picked up a second swab.

Then, to Eli's horror the doctor began swabbing both of the footballer's feet at the same time as Dennis went on tickling the bottom of Eli's left foot...

"OH NO, no, OH NO," Eli squealed crazily. "D-don't you guys tickle both my feet at the same danged time, oh Gawd Doctor Tick Lee..."

As the doctor worked at swabbing the bottoms of Eli's trapped feet and Dennis swab tickled his arches and balls of his feet the young handsome footballer laughed and hawed and bucked involuntarily and sexily under the straps. Eli's tear/laugh filled eyes were suddenly riveted to the doctor's nametag clipped to his white lab coat.

"T-tick, Lee, tick-lee..." Eli whispered under his breath and in between hoots and hollers of laughter. "Ticklee...Ah jeez, your name says it all Doc... if that's really your name that is...Now I know I've been had...HAW, HAW, HAW, HAW, HAW, HAW! F-FUCKING FUCK! Doctor Ticklee is ticklin' me! HA, HA, HA, HA, HAH, HAH, HAH!"

"And such a creative rhyme that is young Eli," the doctor quipped and swabbed Eli's feet harder yet, really making the young man laugh and guffaw.

It was about twenty minutes later when Doctor Tick Lee and Dennis stopped swabbing Eli's feet. The footballer's tootsies were now completely moist and somewhat soggy feeling...

"Hooooo, th-thanks Doc, thanks Dennis, jeez guys, that was some foot cleaning you two just gave me..." Eli said with a grin as the doctor lifted the young man's head and again held the bottle of strange tasting mineral water to his trembling lips.

"Well, that was just the swabbing end of cleaning up your feet young Eli," the doctor said as Eli sipped down the water. "Have another good drink and then we will start the moisturizing and softening of your feet..."

"Er?" Eli asked as he sipped the water.

"Oh yes my dear young man," the sinister sounding doctor said. "We have a way to go before I start examining that twisted ankle of yours... Now, be a good football star and drink up... Somehow I get the feeling that you are going to be very famous someday...so I want to be sure to take good care of you here today..."

As Eli sipped the water he felt his cock stirring more-so in the protective cup under his football uniform knickers, so much-so that as he grew harder and harder and more stiff in the thing he was finding that there was nowhere for his erect cock and churning balls to go.

"Errrr..." Eli said and the doctor took the bottle away from his lips.

"Enough water for now Eli?" the doctor asked.

"Y-yeah, I suppose, I suppose so Doc," Eli said as the doctor capped the bottle and handed it to Dennis who set it back on the table. "S-say Doc, th-that water, it tasted kind of unusual and I gotta admit I'm feeling kind of strange here..."

"Oh? Strange in what way young Eli?" the doctor asked.

"I-I hate to admit this Doc, but I'm harder than steel in my protective cup that I got on..." Eli responded with a sheepish looking grin. "Wh-why'd that water taste so strange?"

"You are wearing a protective cup over your privates?" the doctor asked, looked at Eli's knickers covered crotch and then at Dennis.

"Uh, yes, I uh, didn't get a chance to take it off before Dennis here so gallantly carried me out of the locker room," Eli replied and felt his manhood churn another notch upwards in his cup. "Now, about that water you made me drink..."

"Well, besides water having been in the bottle I added a few supplements to it as well, vitamins and some Chinese herbs," Doctor Tick Lee said with a leering smile.

"S-supplements? Ch-Chinese herbs?" the footballer asked as he felt his sex twitch in his cup with a life of its own. "Oh Gawd, I really, really do get the feeling that I've been had here Doc. I th-think you fed me a Spanish fly of some kind..."

"Hey, that's real clever Eli, a Chinese doctor giving you a Spanish fly..." Dennis chuckled and Eli looked up at him angrily.

"Call it what you will young Eli," the doctor said and picked up one of two bottles marked "Moisturizing Lotion."

Dennis helped himself to a second bottle of the moisturizing lotion...

"OH GAWD no, no, not my danged feet again Doc..." Eli begged through clenched teeth as he struggled fruitlessly under the binding straps and then watched as the doctor and Dennis stepped to the foot of the table, both of them at the same time pouring a liberal amount of the lotion into their hands.

"This lotion is actually a de-sensitizer young Eli," Doctor Tick Lee stated, grinning as the lotion slathered his hands, the sounds of squishing filling the air as the doctor and Dennis coated their hands and fingers with the lotion. "Dennis and I will apply the lotion to hopefully ensure that the tickling sensations you are experiencing will cease. We must keep working on your feet to ensure that that left one is healed by the time your next football game rolls around."

"Oh Gawd, no, no, don't man, please don't lotion up my feet with that stuff," Eli panted, his cock churning and rock hard in his protective cup, his toes wiggling involuntarily at what felt like hundreds of miles per hour.

"What do you mean young Eli?" the doctor asked. "Do you or don't you want us, er, me to tend to your feet, er, your twisted ankle?"

"HAWHAWHAWHAHWHAW..." Eli suddenly erupted into new fits of laughter as the doctor and Dennis's hands and fingers began slathering the lotion onto his right foot first.

The two men were actually taking turns lotioning the star footballer's right foot, their fingers working treacherous ticklish magic at the same time...

The doctor worked both hands over the sides of Eli's foot, moved them to the top, grinding his slicked fingertips against the bottom of the footballer's foot as he did his wicked work...

Dennis then took his turn by lotioning the top of Eli's foot with all ten of his fingers, digging in real deep to the thin flesh as his thumbs pressed hard and swirled against the bottoms of the laughing footballer's meaty feet...

"AAAAAHHHH HAHAHAHAHAHA!" Eli ranted with his head

arched back and his muscular chest heaved upwards under the tight straps holding him fast to the table. "S-some de-sensitizer, what a load of horse shit! HAHAHAHAHAHAHA!"

As Dennis continued to work Eli's right foot with his fingers and thumbs and the lotion the doctor took that moment to slather more lotion onto his hands and proceeded to do the same thing to Eli's left foot. That really made the poor young man haw, haw, haw, and ha, ha, ha even louder yet.

"HAHAHAHAHAHAHA f-fuck, fuck, double fuck fucks," Eli screeched. "D-Dennis, no wonder you brought me here! HAHAHAHAHAHA! You fucking guy, y-you're queer for my big ol' feet! HARHARHAR GAWD, I'm so worked up in my danged cup here Doc! It's as if the ticklin' that you and this so called buddy of mine are doin' to me is making me harder and harder somehow! WHOOOO! HAHAHAHAHA! HAHAHAHAHAHAHA!"

Eli then reeled crazily as the doctor and Dennis slathered both his big bare feet at the same time with the moisturizing lotion...

"HEEHEEHEEHEEEEHEE!" Eli prattled as the doctor and Dennis slicked his toes with the lotion and he nearly flew through the binding straps holding him down when the doctor applied the lotion between his toes. "Y-you guys lied to me! Oh dang it all! That lotion ain't de-sensitizing my big ol' feet, it's makin' them all the more ticklish! HAW, HAW, HAW, HAW, HAW, oh woe is me you guys!"

Dennis saw Eli's frantic reaction as the doctor slicked the lotion between the toes of Eli's left foot and the young man followed suit on Eli's right foot...

Eli reared crazily and bucked wildly under the straps as he laughed himself into a fitful tizzy.

"My, my, my, my, you really are very tickle sensitive aren't you young Eli?" the doctor asked as he and Dennis finished slathering the lotion between the young man's toes. "Even my special lotion didn't stop the tickly sensations it would seem..."

"I-I suppose it's safe to say that I am Doc," Eli muttered as the doctor picked up two bottles marked mineral oil and handed one to Dennis. "OH FUCK, now what?"

"Well, I just want to make sure that your feet are nice and slick when I examine your twisted ankle Eli," the doctor said, grinning fiendishly.

"Yeah, and if I may ask when the hell are you going to do that Doc?" Eli asked.

"As soon as we are done getting your feet prepped young Eli," the doctor said and he and Dennis poured mineral oil over each of Eli's trapped feet. "Thank you Dennis for all your help today…"

"Believe me Doctor Tick Lee, it truly is my pleasure…" Dennis quipped, looking at Eli's foot totally lustfully as he oiled it.

"Yeah, fucker, queer for my feet," Eli whispered through clenched teeth, his head raised and watching as his feet were oiled. "Of all the danged things…"

As the mineral oil dripped on his bare feet Eli felt his hard cock pounding in his protective cup… To the young and handsome footballer it actually looked like cum dripping down and all over his big feet…seeing as the mineral oil was mixing with the moisturizing lotion…making a thick and creamy looking concoction…and all over his feet he thought miserably…

"OHHHHRRRR GAWD, wh-what the fuck did you put in that water Doc?" Eli gasped. "Did you fuckin' drug me man?"

"Are you really all that worked up young Eli?" the doctor asked and glanced over at Dennis.

The two men exchanged a knowing sort of leer…

"I-I sure as fuck am Doc," Eli grunted as the doctor and Dennis began slathering the mineral oil liberally over the handsome footballer's feet, mostly using their fingertips this time.

"AAAHHHAHAHA!" Eli screamed once again. "OH GAWD, y-you

and Dennis are tickling me again Doc!" Oh fucking fucks of all fucks, if my big brother could see me now!"

"As I said, Dennis and I do not mean to tickle you young Eli," the doctor said, not sounding all that sincere as he and Dennis worked the mineral oil over the bottoms of Eli's feet, meanly using their fingertips, working along his arches in unison, on his heels and of course in between his toes. "And the supplements I gave you are by no means drugs. I would not do that to such a promising and up and coming football star..."

"HAHAHAHA, and as I said, I bet you don't mean to tickle my danged feet..." Eli laughed. "Oh fucking fucks...but that sure as fuck is what you all are doing here!"

A while later, after Doctor Tick Lee and Dennis had applied a good amount of the mineral oil to Eli's bare feet the footballer's feet were shiny and slick. With his head raised and supported from behind by the good doctor Eli was forced to chug down more of the aphrodisiac laced mineral water.

"There you are young Eli, a good hearty and cool drink to soothe you after all that laughing you did again," the doctor said and twined his fingers in Eli's silky dark hair.

The young college football star squeezed his eyes halfway shut, his eyes rolled in his head and with each gulp of the water he felt his (cupped) cock engorging more in its protective cup...

"AAAAAAARRRRR jeez Doc, wh-what the fucking fuck is happening to me here?" Eli asked when the doctor again stopped feeding him the fiendish mixture.

"Well, I'm simply getting you ready to have your twisted ankle examined young Eli," the doctor said and when Eli lay his head back down and opened his eyes he saw that the doctor now had a hairdryer aimed at his slicked, oiled and shiny feet.

"H-hey, what's with the dryer Doctor Tick Lee?" Eli asked and his hard cock twitched in its cup prison. "You plan on doing my hair here?"

"Not at all young Eli, this is just to toast, er, dry up your feet of the lotion and the mineral oil that Dennis and I slathered on them..." the doctor explained and clicked on the dryer to the highest and hottest setting. "After I'm done with this Dennis and I will each use a massager on your feet and then I will finally work with that twisted ankle you came here with..."

"Fucking fucks, came here? I feel more like I was kidnapped to here," Eli whispered in the throes of sexual ecstasy. "Dang it all Doc, all you needed to do more than likely was to wrap my ankle in an ace bandage... Fucking totally fucks, Dennis, why'd you bring me here man?"

As the warm sensations from the hair dryer caressed Eli's bare feet he squirmed on the table and sweated some more. He saw on the table next to him a second bottle of mineral water. The footballer wondered fleetingly where that had come from, seeing as he had not seen the doctor or Dennis take it from the refrigerator...but then again, with all the laughing he had been doing he was sure that one of the two men could have taken the bottle from the refrigerator without him having noticed.

When the doctor finished drying Eli's feet he turned the dryer off, set it aside and again fed his handsome patient more of the mineral water. Strapped down the way he was there wasn't much that the college football star could do as he was just about forced fed what he had come to think of as the "Spanish Fly Water." He made churning sounds in his throat with each gulp of the water and his cum chocked balls also churned with each passing second. He swore that he could almost feel his big juicy balls shifting in their sac.

"OHHHHHRRRR fucking fucks Doc, let me off this table so I can use your facilities," Eli bantered desperately. "I really uh, need to take care of some business here..."

"And allow you to possibly injure that ankle some more young Eli?" the doctor quipped. "Why, I would not hear of it... All will be taken care of for you...*and I do mean all Eli*. Now, let's get these feet of yours relaxed yes?"

"NO!" was the loud reply Eli made as the doctor next produced two muscle massagers, handed one to Dennis and each man plugged in their device.

At the sight of the almost dildo shaped devices Eli pursed his lips together and his eyes nearly bugged out of his head. But then, the handsome college football star was off and laughing again as the doctor and Dennis used their dildo shaped muscle massagers on his bare feet. The devices had whirring high-speed axels at their fronts and the doctor and Dennis meticulously and methodically trailed the heads of the axels over and over the bottoms of Eli's feet...the doctor working on Eli's left, injured foot, while Dennis tended to the right sided one.

"HAHAHAHAHAAAAA!" the football player screeched in a high crescendo sounding tone of voice. "OOOOO GAWD of GAWDS! B-by oiling up and lotioning my danged feet you somehow made them even more tick-tick-ticklish! OOOOO you crazy doctor! HAWHAWHAWHAWHA WHAWHAWHAW! You mad scientist! And you tried to tell me that that lotion would de-sensitize my feet, HAR!"

Laughing through clenched teeth and with his head raised again Eli looked down across his strapped down body at Dennis and Doctor Tick Lee. The two men seemed to be lost in some sort of euphoria as they trailed their muscle massagers from the heels of Eli's feet up to his soles, along the backs of his toes and down the fronts of his feet.

"WWWWHHHEEEEEE! HEE, HEE, HEE, HEE, HEE!" Eli laughed, his huge chest heaving under the straps that held him fast. "D-Dennis, th-the coach will get you for this man! HAHAHAHAHAHAHA! Y-you were supposed to take me to the college medical lab! HO, HO, HO, HO, HO, HO, HO, HO, HO! But instead you tricked me and brought me here!"

"He does have a point there Dennis," the doctor said chidingly to Dennis.

"Not to worry Eli, I'll explain everything to the coach..." Dennis said and gripped Eli's toes held his foot fast and dug his muscle massager hard into the epicenter of the bottom of Eli's right foot.

"YAHHHHHHHHHHH! HA, HA, HA, HA, HA, HA, HA, HA, HA, HA, HA, HA!" Eli reeled in crazed laughter.

As Eli laughed and bucked under the straps he felt that his cock was now fully engorged in his protective cup under his football knickers. The helplessly horned up young man arched his head back, licked his trembling lips and laughed, he simply laughed as the doctor and his buddy clicked their muscle massagers up to a higher speed. The sounds of the massagers were like thousands of buzzing flies in the room as they were pressed and trilled and strummed all over his bare feet.

"GAAAAAAAHHHHHHH, ha, ha, ha, ha, ha, ha, ha, ha, ha, ha, ha, ha, I-I need to use the facilities, ha, ha, ha, ha, ha, ha, y-your magic potion that you fed me has gotten the best of me Doc! HA, HA, HA, HA, HA, HA, HA, HA, f-fucking fucks, even my girlfriend doesn't get me this worked up!"

"As I told you young Eli, all will be taken care of *for you...*" the doctor said in a sinister sounding tone. "And I think, seeing as your good friend Dennis here was the one who thought so smartly of bringing you to me, he will be the one to prepare you for when we take care of you...so to speak..."

At the sound of those last words from the doctor Eli looked up at Dennis and the doctor with horror showing in his eyes, yet all he could do was laugh as they electronically massaged his slicked feet...

Eli involuntarily, it seemed, curled his toes back and hee hawed crazily when the doctor and Dennis pressed the tips of the muscle massagers against the balls of his bare feet.

"HA, HA, HA, HA HAW, HAW, HAW!" Eli reeled madly. "Dennis, I'm gonna make sure the coach knows of this man! HAW, HAW, HAW, HAW, HAW, HAW, I-I'm his goddamned golden boy you know, ha, ha, ha, ha, ha, ha, ha, ha, ha, when he finds out what you did to me I'll make sure he throws you off the football team! HAH, HAH, HAH, HAH, HAH!"

"Now Eli, once your ankle is all fixed up you will surely forget all about the uh, ticklish, route we had to take in getting these beautiful feet of yours tidied up," Doctor Ticklee chuckled.

"M-my beautiful feet huh?" Eli screeched in between bouts of uncontrollable laughter. "So that proves it you maniacs, you guys are queer for my danged big feet!"

Then, the doctor and Dennis glided the muscle massagers over and over the very tops of Eli's toes.

"HAAAAAAAAAAA!" was all Eli could say, or spray for that matter at that point.

"Jeez, never knew that the tips of a guy's toes could be so tickle sensitive," Dennis quipped.

"Oh yes my dear Dennis," Doctor Tick Lee said in explanation. "You see, reflexology truly works because every nerve ending, every nerve fiber in the body, it all connects to the feet, to the base if you would. So, with that in mind it stands to reason why young Eli here is chortling in the manner that he is. By pressing on certain areas of the feet it causes other parts of the body to react. That really is what tickling is all about after all..."

"Then in Eli's case at the moment his entire body must be reacting by now..." Dennis laughed and then, with a fiendish look on his face slid his rotating muscle massager back down the bottom of Eli's foot.

Doctor Tick Lee did the same and sweaty and panting Eli screeched his laughter yet again...

"HEE, HEE, HEEEEEEEEEEE, HAR, HAR, HAR, HAR, HAR, HAR, HAR!" was the sound Eli made.

"I must say though Dennis, you were very right when you told me about this young footballer's feet," Doctor Tick Lee said as he moved his muscle massager over and over the bottom of Eli's twitching foot. "They truly are exquisite looking, and so meaty and shapely as well. They really are a man's man feet."

"I KNEW IT, HA, HA, HA, HA, HA, HA, HA, HA!" Eli ranted, his hands curled into fists at his strapped down sides. "D-Dennis, you planned this! You fucker, you are queer for my damned feet! Holy crap! You were just waiting for something like this to happen to me so you could bring me here to this bogus doctor! HA, ha, ha, ha, ha, ha, ha, ha, ha!"

"Oops, looks like I've been found out..." Dennis said snidely and continued tickling Eli's foot with his muscle massager.

"AAAARRRRHHHHHH HAW, HAW, HAW, HAW, HAW!" Eli screeched with his head arched back as the two men swiveled their muscle massagers over and over his wriggling feet.

A short while later, as Dennis worked at wiping Eli's sweat sopped muscular body down with a moistened towel, (seeming to be reveling in his work as he did it) Doctor Tick Lee slowly and gently wrapped an ace bandage around Eli's injured left ankle, leaving his foot exposed however as he did so. The doctor had taken the strap holding Eli's feet down to the table off him in order to get his injured ankle wrapped in the ace bandage.

"A-about time you wrapped up my hurt ankle you nutty doctor," Eli said and then gasped and bucked erotically under the straps over his upper body as Dennis accidentally (on purpose) tweaked one of the footballer's jutted up nipples through the towel he was using to wipe Eli down. "UHHHHHH, GAWD, first my danged feet and now my nips Dennis?"

"Sorry buddy boy," Dennis quipped, smiling leeringly down at his tickled prey.

"Look, lets just let the doc here finish wrapping up my ankle and we'll be on our way okay?" Eli asked and Dennis and the doctor looked at each other quizzically over Eli's strapped down muscular body. "What? Why are you guys looking at each other that way?"

"Well you see Eli, you are under the incorrect impression if you think that simply wrapping your ankle in an ace bandage is what it takes to complete my examination of your injured foot," Doctor Tick Lee said and secured the ace bandage around Eli's ankle with a small metal clip.

"Is, isn't it?" Eli asked and watched miserably as the doctor strapped his feet back down to the tabletop. "Aw Gawd man..."

"Not so young Eli," Doctor Tick Lee said and stood over the footballer as this time Dennis did the honors of feeding Eli the spiked mineral water.

"Aw no, "GLUG"," Eli gasped as he was once more forced to drink down the potent aphrodisiac.

"Not so," Doctor Tick Lee chuckled, sounding very Asian at that moment Eli thought as he chugged down the water. "You see, now I will do a nerve test on your feet. And in order for that test to proceed quickly and efficiently you must, *must*, keep your feet very still. Laughing and moving around while we, er, I, while I am examining the nerves in your feet is not permitted. If you do, do that the test will take longer. Remember young Eli, Dennis and I are not tickling your feet intentionally, although you seem to be under the impression that we are...we are simply proceeding with your treatment."

"You danged quack, you're tryin' to confuse me here," Eli said as Dennis took the bottle from his quivering lips.

"If you think so young Eli, but I assure you that is not the case here," the doctor quickly stated. "However, the more you laugh and squirm and move your feet while the next examination is taking place the longer the test will take, that I assure you of."

Eli looked up at the doctor, gulped hard and felt his juices churning and mixing in his overly inflated nuts.

"Yeah, sure Doc, whatever you say," Eli said sarcastically. "But with you and that so-called buddy of mine tickle tormenting the shit outa my poor tootsies how in hell *am* I supposed to keep them as still as you would like me to?"

"Ah, now that problem is most easily solved young Eli," the doctor said and reached into the pockets of his lab coat.

Eli nearly blanched when he saw the two lengths of rope and the white cloth that the doctor held up...

"Dennis, if you would, please assist me once again," the doctor said and handed Dennis one of the lengths of rope. "We must make sure that Eli does not move his feet even an iota of an inch while we conduct the next test that being the nerve test..."

"Sure thing Doc," Dennis chuckled and stepped to Eli's right foot as the doctor quickly tied the white cloth over Eli's eyes, lifting his head and knotting it in back.

"Hey, what the fucking fucks man?" Eli bantered. "Why are you blindfolding me?"

"It's all part of the test we are about to do young Eli," the doctor said reassuringly and then with his length of rope in hand stepped to Eli's left foot. "Okay Dennis, lets really secure his feet so that they will not move during the next test."

"Yes Doctor Tick Lee," Dennis chuckled.

Eli pursed his lips together when he felt rope being wound slowly and snugly around the sections below his ankles on his feet.

"Wh-what are you guys doin' to me here?" Eli babbled. "Gawd, I hate being without sight, makes me feel real vulnerable."

"Nothing to be worried about young Eli," the doctor said and then he and Dennis pulled the slack of the ropes around Eli's strapped down feet taut and tied the ends of them to the legs of the table at either end. "There, now you will be able to keep your feet totally immobilized during the next test."

"What uh, what exactly does the next test entail Doctor Tick Lee?" Eli asked the feeling of his engorged cock as it churned in his protective cup over the top at that point. "UHHHHHHHHH!"

"Well, its quite a simple nerve test actually young Eli," the doctor said, taking two clicker style ball point pens from the front pocket of his lab coat and handing one to Dennis. "You see, what we are going to do is write on the bottoms of your feet and..."

"WHAT?" Eli grunted, lifting his blindfolded head up off the table. "WRITE on the bottoms of my feet?"

"Well yes, that way we can watch the involuntary twitches your feet and toes make despite the fact that they are now immobilized. You understand I am sure..."

"I understand that that will tickle the tar out of me and I'll be laughing again in no time whatsoever," Eli said pleadingly. "And you said that I can't laugh during this test..."

"That is true young Eli," the doctor reiterated. "And remember, if you do laugh it will make the test time longer."

"Wh-what are you and that buddy of mine going to write on my danged feet?" Eli asked.

"Well, its funny, no pun intended there, funny you should ask that young Eli," the doctor said. "That is what will make the nerve test so much fun."

"I don't understand," Eli said.

"We will write things football related and you have to guess what we have written," the doctor said happily.

"Hey, now that sounds like a great game Eli," Dennis said, and squeezed Eli's right foot.

"Sure, fun for the two of you," Eli responded sarcastically.

"Okay Eli, lets begin yes?" the doctor asked and Eli felt the tips of the pens pressed against the bottoms of his big meaty feet.

"OH GAWD, no, no," Eli pleaded.

"If you guess correctly what we have written Eli and your feet both twitch and all your toes as well then I will know that your left ankle is not broken," the doctor went on explaining. "And you must not laugh either. If however, your feet do not twitch properly and your toes do not move then I will know that there is a problem with the nerves in your feet and more than likely your ankle will need further treatment...although I seriously doubt that...but we do want to be cautious now don't we?"

"I-I suppose so Doctor Tick Lee," Eli said and clenched his hands into fists at his strapped down sides.

"Okay Dennis, lets begin," Doctor Tick Lee said and then Eli felt the pen tips scrawling on the soles of his feet.

He grimaced behind his blindfold, pursed his lips tightly and did all he possibly could not to laugh out loud.

"I-I think, ERRRRRR, I think I feel a letter "Y" not, not sure," Eli said shrilly. "OH GAWD DOC..."

Dennis and the doctor looked at each other evilly, they held tight to the upper parts of Eli's feet and wrote some more on the soles of them.

"O-okay, I think on my other foot I felt a letter "E", Eli said. "And that was an...OHHHHH oh no, no,

PWAHHHHHHHHH HAHAHAHA y-you crazy doctor, you tricked me again...HARHARHARHARHAR!"

"OH dear Eli, now we will just have to continue conducting the test," the doctor said, sounding as if he really didn't feel all that sorry for his patient.

"HAH, HAH, HAH, HAH, HAH, HAH, HAH, HAH, HAH, HAH, HAH, H-how can I not laugh, with what the two of you are doing to my danged feet?"

"Well Eli, if you want this test to be finished soon you won't laugh," Doctor Tick Lee stated sternly and Eli felt his pen squiggling over his foot.

"I-I can't even begin to guess what you two are writing, HAHAHAHAHAHAHAHA!" Eli laughed crazily.

"You know Dennis, I have found that when you tell a ticklish person not to laugh while they are being tickled they will, for some reason, laugh all the harder," Eli heard the doctor say softly to Dennis. "It drives them mad to be told not to laugh...they lose control..."

"So I see," Dennis replied. "So I see..."

The sounds of Eli's mad laugher filled the small room as Doctor Tick Lee and Dennis did their dirty work, writing words like "Young Miss", "Eli", "Quarterback" and "Stadium" on the bottoms of Eli's big feet. A few times the blindfolded Eli could have sworn that he felt the big toe on his right foot being sucked...

Was that possible? Was Dennis that queer for his feet that he would suck his danged toes? As the sucking sensations coursed through his being Eli felt his rage cock oozing pre seed in his protective cup...

"OOHHHHRRRRR HAW, HAW, HAW, HAW, HAW, I-I think that was an "E" that one of you just scrawled on my danged foot..." Eli screeched loudly.

"Now Eli, I must insist that you refrain from that laughter," the doctor said admonishingly. "I really need to be able to concentrate on your feet..."

"Th-that's what I thought you were doing all this time man!" Eli squawked madly and arched his blindfolded head back amid gales of raucous laughter.

Finally, after about an hour's time of writing on the young footballer's feet the doctor was able to determine that Eli's ankle was indeed not broken. Eli managed to stop laughing long enough for the doctor to make that assessment. Although Eli wondered if after all the laughing he had done the doctor decided to take some mercy on him, more likely not though.

"HOO whee, oh God," Eli muttered as Dennis did the honors of taking the blindfold off him as the doctor gently kneaded both his bare written on feet.

"Well Eli, I am sure you are one very relieved footballer right about now, yes?" Doctor Tick Lee asked his patient as Eli lay there panting and catching his breath.

"I-I sure am Doc, I'm real glad my ankle isn't broken after all," Eli said breathlessly. "Do you think I'll be able to play in the next game though?"

"Well, that depends on when the next game is young Eli," the doctor said, continuing to knead Eli's big feet, seeming to be reveling in the task.

Eli's huge cock pounded in his protective cup, almost demanding relief at that point... Standing beside him Dennis gently tousled Eli's sweat sopped hair.

"If the game is more than a week away you can certainly play in it," the doctor said as he cleared up the utensils that had been used to examine/tickle Eli. "I would advise that for the next few days you stay off that foot. If you must go to classes I suggest you go as slowly as possible. It's only a very thin fracture but you still want to take it easy."

"Cool, thanks Doctor Tick Lee, *I guess*," Eli chuckled. "Sorry about all the danged laughing I did..."

"And I'm sorry for having had to tickle you," the doctor replied not all that sincerely, looking at his watch at the same time. "Dennis, I think it best that we finish up now with young Eli here. I have another patient to get to very soon."

"Sure thing Doctor Tick Lee, I'll get the ice," Dennis said happily and stepped over to the refrigerator.

"Th-the ice?" Eli asked, lifting his head up and looking across the room at Dennis as the doctor undid the lengths of rope tethered to the young footballer's ankles, but leaving him strapped down still. "Doctor Tick Lee, why is he getting ice?"

"Well, you see young Eli, since I used various methods to examine and analyze the problem with your ankle your feet are rather heated up at the moment," the doctor said, giving Eli's left foot an affectionate squeeze as he spoke. "Not to mention other heated parts of you..."

Eli shuddered as the doctor looked leeringly at his crotch as he said the last.

"Oh Gawd, what now?" Eli whispered desperately and squirmed under the binding straps.

"Together Dennis and I will cool you down," the doctor went on as Dennis stepped over to the table with a tray of ice cubes. "I will work at cooling your feet down and getting the ink off them while Dennis assists you in; let's call it, other areas, yes?"

The doctor grinned lecherously as Dennis placed the tray of ice cubes on the small table next to the second bottle of mineral water.

"Oh dang, woe is me, you guys Spanish flied me," Eli muttered as the doctor picked up an ice cube and held it in his thin claw-like fingers. "I'm more worked up and sexier feeling than a cat in heat on a hot summer night in New York City..."

"Very apropos way of stating it young Eli," Doctor Tick Lee chuckled and trailed the ice cube he was holding across the tips of the footballer's toes.

"OHHHH NO, no, don't tickle me again, please Doc," Eli bantered and then, with his head still raised watched helplessly as Dennis began unlacing his football uniform knickers. "OH FUCKS, HA, HA, HA, HA, HA, HA, HA, D-Dennis, what are you up to now man? OH GAWD man, no, no, don't be going after my stalk huh buddy?"

Eli, laughing uncontrollably struggled fruitlessly under the straps as Dennis undid the drawstring on his knickers and then slowly lowered them in front.

"HAW, HAW, HAW, HAW, HAW, HAW, HAW!" Eli cackled loudly as the doctor trailed the ice cube up and down the bottoms of his feet alternately. "Fucker, tickling me again! HAHAHAHAHAHA! And my so called buddy, going after my danged baby maker...HAHAHAHAHAHAHAHA!"

"Ah yes Eli, its all so funny, yes...yes..." the doctor said, sounding fiendishly Asian.

Eli made a very pretty and sexy picture as he lay there laughing and now with his football knickers pulled down in front, his protective cup fully on display at his crotch.

"OOOOOORRRRRR HAR, HAR, HAR, HAR, HAR!" Eli crowed

loudly. "D-Doc, pl-please, stop icing up my danged feet..."

With his head still raised Eli saw that Doctor Tick Lee now had an ice cube in each hand and was strumming them up and down the bottoms of his feet at the same time. The young footballer's feet were starting to feel very cold, very cold indeed, almost as if he was laying there with his big feet in an old fashioned icebox.

"Just cooling your dear feet down for you young Eli and then I'll get the ink off for you," the doctor said with a smile.

"HAHAHAHAHA!" Eli screamed laughingly.

Then, to his utmost shock Eli watched as Dennis brazenly undid his protective cup and lifted it off his crotch area, revealing Eli's succulent thick veined and nearly nine inch cock and a pair of the juiciest kiwi sized nuts that Dennis had ever seen.

"OOOOHHHRR GAWD," Eli grunted as his throbbing and purple headed cock sprung straight up and pointed at the heavens, pre cum dripping liberally from his wide and gaping piss slit.

Like a vampire Dennis leaned down and with blinding speed slurped the oozing pre seed from his buddies cock head.

"D-Dennis, do-don't be eating at my cock man," Eli squawked. "HAHAHAHAHA Oh fuck, oh double fucks and woe is fucking me...I'm so fucking horned up that I can't even think straight anymore...HAW, HAW, HAW, HAW, HAW, HAW!"

"Remember what Doctor Tick Lee said Eli," Dennis said with a grin, looking hungrily at his buddies cock and sweaty balls. "All will be taken care of for you. I'll get you thinking straight again buddy..."

Eli saw the doctor take two new ice cubes from the tray and start trailing them now over the tops of his feet, his arches and in between his toes, as the first two cubes he had used had melted away. Eli's feet felt nearly frozen at that point but he was still plentiful ticklish as the doctor did his dirty work.

"Fuck man, I'm goin' to play you like a musical instrument..." Dennis whispered in a man's passion and Eli screamed anew when he looked up and saw that his buddy was holding two long stiff goose feathers.

"OH MY GAWD OF GAWDS," Eli shrilled in between laughing his head off. "D-Dennis, what are you planning on doing with those man? Play me like a musical instrument? This ain't band class here! HAR, HAR, HAR, HAR, HAR, HAR, HAR, oh fuck me, I can't stop laughing!"

Once again the sucking sensations at Eli's big toe had begun again. When he looked downward at his feet he saw that Doctor Tick Lee was in a state of ecstasy as he sucked one of the footballer's big toes, while at the same time using the ice on the bottoms of his feet, cooling them down, tickling them.

"HAH, HAH, HAH, HAH, HAH, HAH, D-Dennis, would you look at that man?" Eli screamed. "Fucking guy is sucking my big toe...WHOOOO WHEEEEE man; I swear I can feel that in my cock and...OHHHHH NOOOOO DENNNISSSSS! NOOOOO!"

The sounds of Eli's laughter reached new heights when Dennis began using the tips of the goose feathers to tickle the captive footballer's nipples tips, his cock and his balls.

"How long do you think it will take him to explode his juices using these feathers on him Doctor Tick Lee?" Dennis asked and Eli sputtered and spat as he laughed and breathed heavily, the sexual feelings coursing through his muscular body at what felt like hundreds of miles per hour.

"Well Dennis, the way we have young Eli so worked up, so tickled, so very well dosed with my potent aphrodisiac, I would say, as you Americans say, it won't be long now," the doctor said and ran ice cubes over the bottoms of Eli's feet in circular motions.

"OOOOHHHH NO, NOOO, you wouldn't...HAHAHAHAHA!" Eli laughed helplessly. "Y-you guys wouldn't make me shoot my load here... WOULD YOU?"

Eli arched his body tautly under the tight straps, really showing off his huge musculature. His cock seemed to engorge all the more when Dennis slid the tip of one of the feathers into his piss slit and twirled it around in there.

"AAAAAAAAAAYYYYYYYYY! WH-what a shitty thing to do to a poor guy's cock," Eli ranted and laughed harder yet as the doctor helped himself to two new ice cubes once again and began icing his feet some more.

"HAH, HAH, HAH, HAH, HAH, HAH, oh you fucking guys, goddamned tricksters!" Eli shrilled.

The sensations on his cock, his balls and his nipples were gentle ticklish sensations holding him perilously balanced on the edge of shooting his load. But in his heart of hearts the young football star knew that it would take more than just the soft touch of feathers to make him shoot his load... and inwardly Eli was desperate, frantically in need of shooting a load...or two or three perhaps. The crown of his cock was actually sweating and twitching as Dennis did his dirty work. A few times Dennis leaned down and teasingly licked and nipped at Eli's jutted up man-sized nipples...

"FUCKER, pervert, stop teasing my nips man," Eli swore. "If you're plannin' on getting me off then lets just get to it huh? HAHAHAHAHAHA I'm about at the end of my rope here Dennis..."

To further Eli's mounting and pent-up sexual frustration Dennis used both his feathers at his football buddies crotch, swirling and twirling them around and around his balls, over his erect cock shaft and in and out of his piss slit...

"AAAAAYYYYYYYY, f-fucker, cock teasing me worse than the time my girlfriend and her two sorority sisters had at me...HAHAHAHA! I-I need to shoot my load you degenerates! PPPFFFFFFFFFF! HAHAHAHAHA! OH FUCKING WOE IS ME can't believe I just said that..."

"Just what I have wanted to hear young Eli," the doctor said and held up the white cloth blindfold. "And now that I am done icing your feet Dennis and I can assist you together in that very private area...yes?"

Eli's jaw dropped and he finally stopped laughing, catching his breath as the doctor approached with the blindfold...

A few moments later Eli was blindfolded and gasping, grunting and heaving breathlessly as his cock was being worked on. It was the only way he could think to put it as he felt something warm, squishy and tight being slid over his most private of areas.

"Oh fuck, wh-what in Sam hell are you guys planning on doing to me next here?" Eli panted. "Wasn't tickling me nearly to death enough for the two of you?"

In response all Eli heard was the sound of sinister chuckling...

The young footballer then gasped breathlessly when he felt what he thought was thin wires being wound around and around his sweaty and cum filled balls.

"HUUUHHHH, holy fuck and woe is me, what am I in for now you guys?" Eli bantered and even though his eyes were covered the young football star's eyes were filled with wonderment and fear as he felt his most private of areas being tended to.

He nearly flew off the table when one of the men gave the root of his manhood a gentle squeeze.

"AAAAAHHHH..." Eli panted.

"Not to worry young Eli, you are in good hands," Eli heard the doctor say reassuringly and then the tip of the mineral water bottle was pressed against his trembling lips. "Now, drink up young Eli, drink up, I assure you, you are going to need it...for what we do to you next you are going to need it..."

Whoever was feeding him the water held his head up as he chugged it down, his Adam's apple bobbing real sexily as he drank. His iced feet were shivering and as he chugged the water his cock seemed to engorge more-so in whatever the squishy device was that it had been slid into...

When the blindfold was taken off him a short while later and Eli saw the device tethered to his cock and balls a look of total disbelief came over his handsome face and he let out a womanly sounding shriek of horror...

"Young Eli, you are about to be, as you American's say, milked like a bull, yes?" Doctor Tick Lee asked, he and Dennis chuckling as poor Eli took in the sight of the gizmo hooked up to his cock and balls, his horror filled eyes trailing over the wires and tubes that led from it and to the plastic containers they were hooked up to.

"Fuckers should have kept me blindfolded..." Eli whispered and laid his head back down on the table...

# DOWN ON THE FARM

## Written by: Dutch Roberts

*So, I think I've known my buddy Travis now longer than any other person on this big ball of dirt. We're like brothers, I tell ya, but that son-of-a-bitch has gone and found himself a girl, which really pisses me the fuck off. I mean, how can he go and do that? Who am I gonna hang out with? Who's gonna be my drinkin' buddy? My fishin' buddy? My fuck buddy?*

*Whoa, wait just a flippin' minute...I know what you're thinkin', ya sick fuck. Travis and I aren't like that. We're not. We have this agreement, ya see. We can fool around, we can fuck around, like animals in heat even, but we're not allowed to grow fond of each other. It's just not right.*

*Well, in these parts it's not.*

*Anyway, the fucker is gettin' married later today, but I'm havin' none of that. He wants me to be his best man and all, well, trust me, he's gonna get the best damn man he'll ever find this side of the Mississippi, and it ain't gonna be in the weddin' sense of the word.*

*Shit, here he comes. I better make myself look busy.*

"Hey, Jack, why aren't you inside getting ready? We need to be at the church in a few hours."

*Oh fuck! Look at him. Will ya just look at him! He's such a fuckin' cock tease. And in that monkey suit, even more so. Shit, he looks good, too good. Damn fucker. He's a cock tease, I tell ya. He most certainly is. Did ya notice how my prick bucked in my jeans just now as he came around the corner? Fuck.*

"Uh, yeah, I know. I just thought I would get some work done before we left. Ya know...the pigs can't slop themselves."

"Huh...I guess you're right. Just don't take too long. Ok?"

"Yeah, yeah. Ok. Ya better get back inside before ya get all dirty."

"Oh, yeah, right. We wouldn't want that."

"Fuck no, Trav, we wouldn't want that at all."

*Shit, just look at him go. He has the sweetest little ass I've ever tapped. I mean, fuck, it's so firm and smooth and...aww, shit, I have to stop thinkin' like this or I'm gonna find myself poppin' a load in my pants right here and now. It's bad enough I'm sportin' this rock hard woody.*

*I wonder if he noticed.*

*Anyway, I can't help wonderin' where it all went wrong. I mean, we have a really good thing goin' here, Travis and I do, but somewhere along the way he decided it wasn't good enough for him. Let me tell ya somethin', this farm his parents left him, it's makin' a killin' havin' the two of us workin' on it. A real fuckin' killin'. That's because we both bust our asses hard every single day, from sun up to sun down. Shit, I know I'm not the brightest bulb or the sharpest knife, but, come on, I can hold my own. I'm a hard worker. I also know what it takes to make someone happy and, ya know what, I look pretty fuckin' good in and out of my jeans too. Put me in one of those damn tuxes and you'll see. Workin' on a farm can do that to ya, ya know. It does a body good and let me tell ya, mine is one hot slab of prime beef. Travis' is too... if ya were wonderin'.*

*So, wanna hear my plan?*

*Ok. I thought ya would.*

*Ya see, Travis and I aren't gonna make it to the church on time. Not even close. I plan on workin' out here all mornin', and when he comes back out to get me rollin' along, I'm gonna put up a little fight. Then, when he's good and angry, I'm gonna show him a thing or two. I'm gonna remind him of what he's givin' up by goin' off and gettin' married.*

*Stupid pisser.*

*Hold on a minute... let me strip out of this flannel shirt. Damn it's gettin' real hot out here.*

*Ok, there, that's better. Phew, much better. That breeze comin' off the lake feels good. Real good. I love when it runs through my damp hair and wet pits. It sort of tickles, ya know? Kind of reminds me of the times Travis and I have gone skinny dippin'...oh, yeah...those were some hot summer days, they were. Shit. We've had some great times together...*

*Hmm, where was I? Oh, yeah, right...my plan!*

*Boy, I can't wait to get my hands on him and that hulkin' body of his. I plan on workin' him over real good, real good indeed. He won't know what hit him until he's takin' it deep inside that sweet ass of his.*

*Shit, he's comin' right back! Fuck.*

"Hey, Jack, sorry to keep bothering you, but...well, do you have a minute? I need to ask you something."

"Sure, Trav, shoot."

*Boy, look at him, he's lookin' so fuckin' hot. His shoulders look huge in that get up...and his waist. Fuck! I think it's shrunk since yesterday. Did he get a haircut too? Damn, his thick, blond locks look real neat and pretty.*

"So, I'm just wondering...are you pissed off at me?"

*Fuck. He knows. I'm gonna have to lie to him. Boy, do I hate lyin'.*

"Uh, no. Why would ya think that, Trav? I could never be mad at ya. Honest."

*Asshole.*

"Are you sure? Because, well, you seem miles away...distant, you know, and, well, Jack...you know you mean the world to me."

*Fuck. Why's he tellin' me this now? He's gonna ruin everything.*

"Trav, really, I'm cool. Don't worry about me."

*Ya jerk off.*

"Ok, if you say so. I just want to make sure you're ok with this."

*Damn, why is he comin' closer? Oh fuck, he smells so good. Shit, are those new shoes too? Boy, they look nice on his big, sweet feet. God, I want to suck on his toes now too!*

"I'm good man. Honest."

*Oh fuck! No. Don't...oh shit, his touch sends chills up my fuckin' spine every single time. And he's only touchin' my shoulder! Fuck. I must be really horned up today!*

"Good, Jack, I'm glad to hear that. Really I am. I would never want to hurt you."

*Oh, man, no...is he makin' a move on me?*

"Yeah, we're cool."

*Shit. He's lickin' his lips! He's gonna...hmm, yeah, hmm.*

*Oh, God! His lips feel incredible! They're so soft, but...strong, and firm. Shit, so firm. I think my cock's gonna rip right through my jeans. Oh man, he's slidin' his tongue inside my hungry mouth! Is that his hand on my fly? Fuck! He's undoin' my jeans!*

"Trav, oh man..."

"Shh, Jack, don't speak."

*Oh man, his hands feel amazin'! The way he's holdin' my cock...oh man.*

*What? What did he just say?*

"Earth to Jack, listen up, I need you to take your boots off."

"Uh, sure...yeah, whatever ya want Trav."

*Oh fuck...how am I goin' to focus on takin' my boots off when he's got me by the family jewels? Oh man, his hands feel so smooth...and warm. So freakin' warm. Shit, he sure knows how to handle me. I'm like putty in his hands. Oh, thank God, he's stopped playin' with the boys.*

*Fuckin' tease.*

"There ya go, Trav. Off with the boots...and the jeans too! Just like ya want them."

*Damn, how is it that I'm standin' here buck ass naked, when it was goin' to be the other way around? Just look at him!*

*Smug bastard.*

"Ok, Jack, now, I need you to head on into the barn."

"Uh, sure, Trav."

*God, why do I always do everything he tells me to? Huh, well, I guess it's because he looks so good doin' it. Shit, he looks good enough to eat in that sharp suit of his. And I can't get over how good his hair looks. And those shoes! Woof!*

"There we go. Now get up onto that workbench."

"Sure, Trav. Whatever ya want man."

*Now, what the hell does this fucker have in mind? We've never played like this before.*

"Ok, Jack, now, you trust me...right?"

"Trav, what sort of stupid ass question is that? Ya know I trust ya."

*What the heck is goin' on here?*

"Ok, just checking, because, well...I'm going tie you to this workbench. Ok?"

"Sure."

*What the fuck? When did he get into this sort of crazy shit?*

"Great. That's perfect Jack."

*Oh man, he's serious. Look at him go! Where the heck did he get all of that rope? Oh shit, he's trussin' me up like a fresh buck on the hood of my truck! Where the heck did he learn how to tie someone up like this? Sure, he's helped me bag a few critters, but this is totally different.*

*Right?*

*Damn, there go my socks!*

"Ok, that's it. Good and tight...but not too tight, right?"

"No, Trav, not at all."

*Ya wild fuck.*

"Now, as you can see, I have your little piggies tied just so, right out in the open so I can see them real good."

"Uh, yeah, why is that Trav?"

"Because, well, I don't think I've ever told you this, Jack, but those little bastards have been driving me wild for years now."

"Really?"

*Wow...really?*

"And, so, I figured, why not take the time to enjoy them before I tie the knot?"

"Shit, Trav, ya didn't need to rope me up to do that. All ya had to do was ask."

"Hmm, I don't know Jack, you're pretty ticklish. Remember last week, down at the lake?"

"Yeah, so?"

"Well, I plan on really enjoying them...I mean, *really* enjoying them."

*Oh fuck. What the hell does this fucker have in mind?*

"Oh yeah?"

*Man, I'm screwed.*

"Yeah."

*Shit. Where's he goin' now?*

*Oh, ok. He's back.*

*What the hell is that in his hand? Is that a bucket of...?*

"Honey ok with you, Jack?"

"Uh, sure..."

*What the hell does he plan on doin' with that?*

"Cool, because I love the taste of it, Jack, almost as much as our goats do."

*Oh man, he's...drippin' it all over my feet! What the fuck? Oh shit. He's... lickin' it off! Oh God, that feels amazin'! Oh man, now...he's...suckin' on my toes! He's slurpin' the honey out from between them! Oh, God, this feels incredible!*

"Ha!"

"Hmm, yeah, you like that? Huh? That feels real good, doesn't it Jack?"

"Ha! Ha!"

*Shit. Ya have no idea fucker! No idea! Oh man, he's...suckin' each toe, one at a time. Fuck, he's really givin' them a good tongue lashin'. Dear God, look at what its doin' to my cock!*

"Hmm, oh yeah, so sweet. That's my Jack."

*Oh fuck! Does he have any idea what his mouth is doin' to me?! Oh, fuck, yeah, I guess he does by the way he just gripped my piece of meat. Oh man! Now he's strokin' and suckin' me?!*

"HA!"

"Yeah, that's it boy, let it all out. Tell me how much you like me sucking on your toes!"

"Oh, fuck, Trav...ha...it's incredible man! It's so...ha...fuckin' amazin' man!"

*Jesus Christ, this fucker knows his shit. Damn, just look at him go. He's a fuckin' foot pig and he's drivin' me...*

"HA! HA!"

"Yeah, that's it. Let me hear how much you love this."

"HA! HA! OH FUCK! I do man. I love it!"

*This is crazy! Why would he wanna give this up for that girl? Just look at his face! He's in heaven! He's in fuckin' foot heaven, suckin' on my big toes.*

"That's right, Jack, show your big bro how much you want him to continue. Let that pre flow, boy! Let it flow!"

*Oh fuck! I'm oozin' like a fuckin' fountain. Just look at that stream! My fuckin' cock is goin' to explode if he keeps this up! Oh man! His mouth feels...like... oh, God...no!*

*Here it comes!*

"Yeah! That's it babe, shoot that hot, thick load! That's it! Let it go!"

*Oh man...yeah!*

*Shit.*

*I can't stop! He's still suckin' and lickin' and strokin' and I can't stop!*

"Damn, Jack, you're out of control! Just look at that fucking geyser of jizz! Phew, you almost got some on me man. Damn, you must have been saving up that load for a few days now."

*Yeah, fucker, and ya were goin' to take it up that sweet ass of yours, but ya went and ruined my whole plan.*

*Well, sort of...*

"Ok, well, I have to get running Jack, or I'm going to be late getting to the church."

*Huh, what? Did he just say something about church? He's still goin'?*

"But, don't worry...I'm going to leave you in good hands."

*What? Wait!*

"No, Trav...don't go."

"But, I have to Jack. You know that. I'm just sorry you're not going to be there to see my big day. It's going to be a really special moment for me and Lara."

"What? But..."

"Jack, come on, we both know you can't come to the church. You'll make a scene."

"No, I won't. I promise."

*Ok, maybe I would make a fuckin' scene, but it would be because I...*

"Aww, come on, don't make this hard on me, Jack. You have to stay here."

"But...no...please."

*Why won't he listen to me? Why is he still goin'? How do I get him to understand that I...?*

"Ok, I have to run buddy. Be good. Ok, Jack? I'll send someone over later to untie you."

"Sure."

*Oh man, is he gonna...oh man, those lips! And...I can still taste the honey! Oh God, why does this have to end? Why Travis? Can't ya feel it too?*

*Why?*

*Shit, he's leavin'. This is it. No more good times with my buddy Travis. My hot, fuck buddy, Travis.*

*Wait a minute.*

*What's that noise?*

*Oh fuck. He didn't.*

*No.*

*Oh fuck no! He let the fuckin' goats out! Oh God! No! They can smell the honey! Oh God! Here they come! My feet are still covered...oh God...no...*

"HA! HA! HA!"

*Damn, I love ya man.*

# TICKLE 'EM ALMER

## Written by: Anonymous Cop

Mahoney's Grille couldn't be classified as an actual "cop bar" even though a lot of the city's police officers went there after a tour of duty to wind down with a beer or two. Sergeant Harry Waldis liked it because the women there weren't the usual cop groupies of other cop bars and he could pick up some good looking divorcee or straying wife for a quick fuck. Harry had the looks and the lines to sweet-talk just about any woman he cast his eyes on. The sergeant was just a shade over 6 feet, a sturdy 185 pounds of fat free muscle, the rugged jaw of movie heroes, and those dark blue penetrating eyes which seemed to look right into a woman's soul. Yes, Harry had everything a female on the make could want. However, with all these assets Harry did have one glaring debit, a wife at home. Harry had married Marie two years earlier thinking it would help his career if he had the image of a wife and solid home life on his resume. It wasn't that Harry didn't love Marie, in his own egocentric way, he was very fond of her, but Harry firmly believed that no woman should be deprived of his manhood and after a few months of complete faithfulness to Marie, Harry started playing the field. He was relatively discreet about his trysts but let's face it even the dumbest wife can tell when her hubby is playing around.

Harry hadn't spotted any potential conquests in Mahoney's but figured it was still early and hope springs eternal, he thought. He was sipping on a beer, looking around at the customers, when he spotted his brother-in-law Tony come into the place in company with his foreman Bear. Tony owned and operated one of the biggest construction companies in town and had worked his way up from laborer to owner in no time. Of course his connections in the Italian community helped along with his reputation of being a tough but honest man. Although he ran the company he still spent a lot of time out on the work sites overseeing and actually doing grunt labor himself, which he justified as his way of keeping in shape. And Tony was indeed in good shape, even Harry the gym rat, admired his physique. His foreman and right hand man, Bear, was a big barrel-chested Italian with hands so large and powerful that, so the story ran, he could squash baseballs by just squeezing them. Few people knew that his real name was actually Almer, and a few close buddies called him Al, but just about everyone else called him Bear, or behind his back, The Silent Bear, as he was a man of very few words.

The two men came up to Harry. "Hey brother-in-law, what are you doing here? Aren't you working tonight?'

Harry nodded to them, "Just got off duty Tony and thought I'd stop in for a quick beer before heading home. Marie is off to your parents for the night so no need to hurry home."

"Yeah, I heard she was visiting Ma for the weekend. Hey let me get you a beer."

Harry knew that any chance he had of picking up something at the bar that night were over with the arrival of Tony and the silent Bear but figured what the hell why not use the time to bond with his in-law. Harry was drinking Bud and preferred it right out of the bottle. The three men stood at the bar chatting about the local sports teams and one beer followed another. Since Tony was paying, Harry never noticed the small white pills that Bear slipped into his beer before handing them over. It wasn't too long before Harry began to feel a little dizzy and drowsy and soon he was having trouble standing.

"Hey Harry, looks like you've had one too many here. Better not be driving, would be something for a Sergeant in the police department to get arrested for DUI. Come on, we'll drive you home."

They carried the now uncoordinated cop between them to their car in the parking lot and by the time they opened the rear door to shove Harry in, he was totally unconscious. Tony laughed, "Fuckin' wimp can't hold his booze."

Harry didn't know what had happened to him when he finally came to. He tried to move to rub his head in the hopes of soothing a head ache but found he couldn't. He was in his own house, stripped naked on his own bed with his arms out-stretched and his wrists tied tightly to the upper bed posts. He legs were stretched out and his ankles tied just as tightly to the bed railing at the end of the bed, with each of his size 11 feet protruding over the rail. Harry thought "what the fuck? Where am I? What happened?" as he struggled to free himself. No luck, whoever had tied him was an expert and it was obvious Harry wasn't going anywhere. Just then the door of the bedroom opened and Tony and the Bear walked in.

"Well, well, my tough acting hard ass cop, it looks as if you got yourself in a bad position."

"What the fuck is going on?" Harry yelled. "Untie me you assholes. This isn't funny."

"Harry, Harry, Harry. Shut the fuck up and listen to me. You have a lesson to learn and we're here to teach it to you."

"Lesson? What lesson? What the fuck are you talking about Tony?"

Tony sat on the edge of the bed so he was looming directly over the bound cop. "Well, Harry, my sister Marie came to see me and she is a very unhappy woman. She says that you are cheating on her. Now Harry that's not nice! Men in our family don't cheat on their wives."

"Bullshit," Harry bluffed, hoping he could talk his way out of this. "Marie is imagining things. I never touched another woman. She's..."

But he never got to finish the sentence because Tony clamped his hand over Harry's mouth, then lifted it and with a full swing, slapped Harry's face hard.

"Aggrrrrrrrr..." Harry moaned.

"Now shut up and listen to me you self centered asshole," Tony continued. "If you open your mouth again except to answer my questions, you'll get worse. Do you understand?"

"This is crazy," Harry shouted but didn't get any further as Tony slammed his fist into Harry's stomach effectively shutting the cop up.

"Now tell me Harry, have you been screwing other women?"

"No, no honest" Harry managed to moan.

"Oh Harry, why do you lie? I know you've been running around. I've had some of my boys watch you at that bar and seen you go off with other dames. Now that's not a nice thing to do to my sister Harry.

"You know Harry, Marie really loves you; damned if I know why she'd love a two-faced skunk like you, but then there is no accounting for women's tastes. And you've made her very sad Harry. She told me all about how you used to make love to her but that you haven't touched her in awhile. She's heart broken Harry.

"You know she told me a lot of things about you Harry. She was reminiscing about the early days of your marriage, about your habits, about your likes and dislikes. One thing she told me Harry was that you are very ticklish. Is that true, Harry, are you ticklish?"

Harry's body stiffened in his bondage and he momentarily panicked. He knew that he was indeed ticklish and that he hated just the thought of being tickled. He didn't answer his brother-in-law, just stared at him.

"Well Harry, Bear here is an expert at tickling people...he is the one who tied you down like this. So I promised him he could have a go at you as a means of teaching you a lesson. Hope you enjoy it as much as I'm sure Bear will. I'm gonna get myself a beer now but holler if you need me Harry." With that Tony left the room chuckling to himself.

Bear approached the bed and looked down on Harry, smiling while he did. He lightly ran his fingers over Harry's hairy chest and up his arms. Harry twitched and jerked at the touch of Bear's hand on his body and if his mind had been clearer he would probably have marveled that such a big man with those huge paws could be so gentle.

"Look Bear, please, just untie me. Don't do this to me, please." Harry pleaded.

But Bear just grinned and went to the end of the bed. He began gently rubbing one of Harry's bound feet and then began playing with each of Harry's toes. Harry's feet were the perfect shape and each toe stood out in apparent independent arrogance. Bear massaged each toe gently and even leaned down and ran his tongue up and down them. At first Harry found the feeling pleasant, but then Bear moved from the toes to the smooth, white skin of Harry's soles and slowly began to tickle them. Harry went wild. The tingling, torturous sensation went right through Harry's body and he jerked and twisted trying to get free, laughing, crying and moaning all at the same time. It was like a hyena being tortured. Soon Bear was working both feet simultaneously, one with each hand – his fingers lightly moving up and down the tortured sole searching for the most vulnerable spots. Harry was going mad, screaming, laughing, moaning, trying to beg Bear to stop but no sensible words came out of his mouth.

Just as quickly as Bear had started, he stopped. Harry let his body settle back into the bed happy for the reprise, his eyes closed, panting and gasping for breath, his muscular body beginning to sweat. Then he sensed Bear was back at his feet and he opened his eyes to see Bear standing there, grinning wider than ever, with what appeared to be a small feather duster in his hands. Harry immediately grasped what was about to happen and screamed, "No Bear, no please. Don't do this."

But along with being silent Bear could just as well have been deaf because the big man paid no attention to the struggling bound cop. He started the feathers slowly on Harry's exposed soles and at once he had the cop jerking and withering in joyful agony...at least from the laughing it seemed it should have been joyful. Bear kept up the action for a long period and Harry thought, when his brain functioned well enough to think, that he couldn't stand any more, and then Bear suddenly switched to Harry's exposed balls. Harry had never had anyone tickle his crotch before and was shocked to find out that that part of his anatomy was equally, if not more so, ticklish than his feet. He was screaming even louder now. Bear played with Harry's balls and cock for a long time, listening with joy to the screams and moans from the helpless cop, and then he attacked Harry's armpits. Bear used both the feather duster and his talented fingers to torture and torment the hapless victim.

Harry was screaming, moaning, panting, swearing, laughing, twitching, turning, jerking, twisting and begging when Tony walked back into the room. Tony stood there watching his foreman methodically work over his brother-in-law's now sweat drenched body, smiling that the smug cop was getting his due. Bear noticed his boss standing there and handed the feather duster to him, indicating without saying anything that Tony should work on Harry's pits while the Bear returned to Harry's feet. Harry was now being attacked from two different angles and the torture was too much for him. His laughter and moaning turned into full fledged crying, the tears pouring down his cheeks. He was begging them to stop but the words were jumbled and unintelligible.

Finally Tony signaled Bear to stop. He sat on the bed next to Harry and said; "Now brother-in-law I'm going to ask you those questions again. If you continue to lie to me then Bear will have another go at you. So I suggest you start owning up to your sins now pal."

Harry just moaned and nodded his head yes.

"Have you been running around on your wife, screwing other women?"

Harry nodded.

"No boy, I want your answers aloud, I'm recording this. And call me Sir when you speak, understand?"

"Yes Sir"

"Ok that's better boy, now tell me Sergeant Harry Waldis of the X-ville Police Department, have you been running around on your wife and screwing other women? Speak up boy."

"Yes Sir."

"Do you think this was a nice thing to do to your wife, boy"

"No Sir.

"Now tell me what women you fucked, what are their names."

"I don't know SIR, just women I picked up in bars."

With that response Bear began tickling Harry's exposed soles once again and the cop screamed out in agony.

"Now, now Harry, isn't it true that you actually have screwed your lieutenant's wife...and a couple of the wives of the patrolmen in your precinct?"

Harry, knowing what would happen if he lied again, said, "Yes SIR, I did screw Lieutenant Harrison's wife."

"And who were the wives of other cops, boy, name them."

And Harry did. He named six different wives of cops who he had laid over the last year; and the names of other women in the city whose husbands were not ones to forgive easily. Tony smiled as he recorded this confession.

"OK Harry, here's the deal. From now on the only woman you touch is your wife Marie. You will devote all you time and attention to her and you will see that she has babies. All Italian women should have babies. And if Marie tells me that you have been anything but the most wonderful, loving, caring husband in the world, then copies of this tape gets sent to the husbands of the wives you named here. And let's face it Harry, these guys ain't gonna be happy about this."

Harry sighed and sunk back further into his bed. He knew when he was beaten. But better this than more of Bear's tickle torture. He knew he couldn't stand up to the big man again.

Tony continued, "Oh Harry don't you think you should thank Bear for taking the time from his off work hours to be with you. By the way, those of us who know him well call him Tickle 'em Almer."

Bear actually chuckled at that statement.

"Yeah Harry I think you should thank him."

Thanking Bear for the torture he had suffered was the last thing in the world Harry wanted but he was still tightly tied and at their mercy so he knew he had no choice.

"Thank you Bear" he said.

"Ah Harry, what kind of a thank you was that? You should really be appreciative of what he has done for you. Do you know that Bear loves to have his cock sucked? Oh yeah, he does. If you were really thankful Harry you'd offer to suck it for him."

Harry panicked. "No, no, I don't do that. I'm no queer." He said.

"Ah Harry, we'll give you a choice. Ask Bear to either continue tickling you or to let you suck his cock; whichever you prefer."

Harry knew he couldn't take more of Bear's tickling but the thought of having another man's cock in his mouth was equally repulsive. He was torn. He looked up to see Tony twirling the feather duster in his hands and grinning and Harry knew what his choice would be.

"Bear Sir can I please suck your cock SIR?" he asked.

Quicker than you could think about it Bear had his pants and briefs off and climbed up on the bed, straddling the bound cop. Harry couldn't believe the size of the monster man tool dangling before his eyes.

"My god," he said, "I can't take that...it's too big...he'll choke me to death."

"Open your mouth Harry," Tony ordered and without thinking Harry did. That was all that Bear needed and in a flash his over 10 inch beer can cock was in Harry's mouth. "Better keep your teeth off that cock if you know what's good for you Harry, but otherwise enjoy it boy."

And Bear started in, slowly, expertly sinking his cock into Harry's throat, letting the cop adjust his throat muscles and letting in enough air so he didn't suffocate. Harry was too stunned to be repulsed and soon felt Bear gently moving his cock in and out of Harry's throat. Then the thrusts became faster and fiercer and before Harry could do anything about it Bear was viciously face fucking the cop. Lucky for Harry it didn't last long. Bear had been hard and ready once he started the tickling on Harry's feet, so his cum was at the edge and ready. And it flowed, wave after wave of warm sticky cum poured from his cock right into Harry's throat. Harry had no choice but to swallow it. Eventually Bear ran out of man fluid and pulled out, but not without making Harry lick his cock head clean first.

Harry was too stunned and humiliated to do anything more than just lay there breathing hard and softly moaning. He was a beaten man.

Tony stood at the bedside looking down on his brother-in-law. "Well Harry I hope you've learned your lesson. From now on you will be the perfect husband ... or else this tape...well you know. You will spend every, you get that Harry, EVERY night at home with Marie. I take that back, no not every night. On Wednesdays you will join me, Bear and some of the other guys in my crew for poker. Marie won't object since she knows you'll be with me. But while the boys and I are playing poker Harry, you'll be serving us our beer, cleaning our boots, and sucking any of the cocks that will be hanging out under the table. You'll learn to really love Wednesday night boy. Now after I take some digital photos of you Harry, Bear will free your hands and you can undo the feet yourself. Have fun and see you next Wednesday."

Bear cut the rope from the bed posts and the two men left the room, both laughing while the now humbled cop lay there, knowing that his days of freedom were over.

# MARK'S REVENGE (OR MAYBE NOT)

## Written by: Christopher Trevor

Christopher's doorbell rang at exactly 6:10 PM that Friday evening, an evening that if he had planned it would never have happened in a million years. At least that's how the author of sinister erotic fiction had always thought his life seemed to be mapped out. When he planned things they often never came to fruition. It was those rare times when fate stepped in that Christopher really enjoyed the rewards that life had to offer. When the doorbell rang a second time Christopher made his way to the window that faced the front of the house from his second floor apartment. The author wasn't expecting anybody that evening so he figured it was either someone ringing the wrong doorbell, (it seemed to the author that whenever someone came to visit his next door neighbor they always inadvertently rang his bell) or perhaps it was some religious devotees pedaling their wares and their word. God knew it was always the season for that. (No pun intended.) Christopher opened the window and looked down at the doorstep. There, under the light of the early evening sun as it went down, standing on his doorstep with his navy blue pinstriped suit jacket hanging over his arm was...

"Mark!" Christopher called downward as his buddy looked up at him as he looked out the window.

"Hey there Christopher, how are you man?" Mark replied, looking up at Christopher. "I realize this is sort of impromptu but I was in the area and I've wanted to talk to you for a while now. Do you suppose you could take a half hour or so and we could do that, *talk* that is?"

The way Mark said the word "talk" made Christopher realize that his buddy was sort of angry, and given what he and his partner had done to Mark the last time he had been to visit them he didn't wonder at the handsome guy's triteness. Christopher saw the way the guy was sweating in his business attire, his burgundy necktie was pulled down and he had the first couple of buttons on his white dress shirt unbuttoned. New York City was known for the worst summers when it came to the high temperatures and the stifling humidity. Mark, like most other office workers could usually be found minus his suit jacket and his tie askew when leaving the comfort of his air conditioned office.

"Sure, we can talk Mark," Christopher said, smiling warmly.

"I mean, if it's a bad time, I realize you're probably busy writing and all, we can make it another time and..." Mark began, standing there looking real sweaty yet oh so sexy in his business attire.

Christopher smiled and said he would be right down to open the door...

Mark stood on the steps sweating; he used an oversized white cloth handkerchief to wipe his forehead and the top of his closely cropped head. As he wiped the sweat off his nearly bald dome he clenched his teeth as he recalled Christopher making sport with that dome last time he was there to visit...and what a visit it had turned out to be Mark fumed. When the door opened he and Christopher looked at each other, Christopher looking at Mark happily, Mark looking at Christopher not equally as happy.

"So, what brings you here...and after work at that?" Christopher asked as he gave Mark's tie a playful tug as he stepped into the hallway.

"I'll explain upstairs," Mark said as he tromped past the author and made his way up the single flight of stairs.

"Hmm, I can tell that this is going to be an interesting conversation," Christopher said, watching from behind as he climbed the stairs as Mark's suit pants rode up, displaying his slip-on (slip-on, always slip-on shoes with this guy) highly polished wing-tips and his long ribbed navy blue nylon dress socks.

Christopher noted how the guy did not wear low cut shoes to the office. No, for the office Mark was much more conservative. But the author thought how even the slip-on wingtips he was currently wearing could be popped off those sexy feet with no problem whatsoever. Once in the apartment Mark stepped to the living room, tossed his suit jacket over a cushioned chair and watched as Christopher locked the door to the apartment.

"Man, it's hot in here, what's the matter, you don't believe in air conditioning?" Mark asked, twisting his already askew tie.

"My air conditioner broke, I have a guy coming tomorrow to fix it, I hope," Christopher replied, stepping into the living room and facing his buddy. "If he can't fix it I'll have to buy a new one..."

"Jeez, how do you get any writing done?" Mark asked and unbuttoned another of his shirt buttons.

"Well, I have a fan set up next to the PC in the other room so its not really that bad, and the air conditioner in the bedroom works okay," Christopher explained. "You can uh, loosen up a bit if it's too hot in here for you. I don't mind if you're wearing just your t-shirt."

"I'll loosen up, but I don't wear t-shirts," Mark said as he unknotted his tie, took it off his dress shirt and tossed in on the chair along with his suit jacket.

"So, you busy at work?" Christopher asked.

"Never mind the nicey nices Christopher, like I said, I was in the area, I had stopped by to visit a friend and then I figured we could talk you and I... and that partner of yours as well," Mark said, almost seething as he unbuttoned his white dress shirt, displaying one of the most beautiful chests, washboard abs and meaty nipples that the author had ever seen.

"Hmm, I didn't know that you had another friend who lives in this area," Christopher said as Mark left his shirt dangling outside his suit pants and then reached into his suit pants pocket for his oversized white handkerchief.

Mark used his handkerchief to wipe the sweat from his robust chest and nipples.

"Jeez, it's beyond hot in here, first time I ever had to visit someone with my shirt hanging open," Mark mumbled. "And what the fuck right Christopher? We're not standing on formality here. But yeah, I do, I have another friend who lives in this area, and he's a real friend, compared to you that is…"

"Hey, that hurt, what did I ever do that you're so angry at me?" Christopher asked.

"Well, let's think Christopher," Mark stated, stepping close to the author and trying his best to really get in his face. "What happened the last time I came here to visit with you and that partner of yours? Speaking of him, where is Adam?"

"He's uh, away on business for his job," Christopher said. "Say, can I get you a cold drink or something? You look like you could use it."

"I'm fine, and I'm not staying long enough for a drink," Mark responded and stepped even closer to Christopher as he spoke. "Now, answer my question, BUDDY, what did you and Adam do to me last time I came here to visit you?"

"We uh, we tickled you," Christopher said, sounding a bit nervous now.

"You tickled me, HA, *you tickled me,*" Mark replied sarcastically. "Was that all you did to me?"

"Well, I suppose we could escalate it a bit and say we *tickle* tortured you," Christopher said. "We locked your wrists behind you in leather restraints and tickle tortured you buddy."

Mark pursed his lips in a sarcastic looking smile and nodded his head before he spoke again.

"Besides the fact that you and that partner of yours tickle tortured the fucking fucks out of me how about the fact that he sucked my nipples till I thought he would chew the fucking nubs right off my chest?" Mark drawled. "That wasn't part of the plan, if, IF, I remember correctly that is. How about the fact that you sniffed my ass? Jeez, but that was sleazy and mortifying, standing there tied up while you made like a dog in heat at my crack. How about the fact that you made sport of rubbing my dome and slathering your mangy tongue over it? GOD! And you fucker, you blindfolded me for most of it...you knew how hyper ticklish sensitive I am and hindering my sight only made me cackle till I thought I wouldn't be able to breathe while I laughed my head off...GOD! You know Christopher, the way I was laughing so loud and so uncontrollably most other guys would have taken the damned blindfold off me at least..."

"Mark, if you remember, and I hope you do, you had agreed to be a tickle slave for me and Adam that day, you set up the scene yourself, please remember that you said that once we had you stripped to your sheer black socks, your slip-on shoes and your underpants and had your hands restrained behind you that you would *pretend* you had changed your mind," Christopher stated, wanting so badly to steal a suck or two or three on Mark's very erect looking nipples. "You said you would *pretend* to have changed your mind and try to go and get your clothes where you had left them after stripping down..."

Mark again smiled through his pursed lips...

"Okay my so called buddy, and if you recall, IF, you recall once you and Adam did have me restrained and while you were feeling me up, grabbing my ass and sucking my nipples I told you that I had really, I HAD REALLY changed my mind..." Mark bantered, sweating more-so now in the heat of Christopher's living room. "Don't you suppose that once I told you I had really changed my mind that the kind thing to do would have been to free my hands for me? But no, I had to start making my way to where my clothes were with my hands restrained behind me, hoping you would come after me to let me loose. But no, instead you came after me to stop me from getting dressed. You and that partner of yours grabbed me and forced me back to your bedroom where you tickle tortured the fucking fucks out of me. You blindfolded me so I wouldn't stand a chance. And then the two of you lifted me like I was a sack of laundry so my slip-on shoes would fall off, you knew how much I would hate my shoes falling off my feet. GOD! And then you and he carried me into that bedroom and...and even though I was blindfolded I knew it was you who had me by the feet while you and Adam carried me, I knew, because I know how much you love my feet in dress socks...and lets face it Christopher, you left my nylon dress socks on me the entire time knowing just how the sheer material against my feet while being tickled would send me through the goddamned roof...Jeez, how many damned hours did you guys tickle me for?"

"Mark, you need to calm down buddy," Christopher said as he watched Mark again wipe himself down with his handkerchief as he sweated more-so. "You're really working yourself into a lather here. Now listen to me. You had said you would pretend to try to get away, and we had set up a safe word so that if you really did want the scene to stop we would have stopped...but you supposedly forgot the safe word. When I asked you the safe word you screamed that you had forgotten it. I thought you said that as part of the scene we were playing out buddy..."

"I did forget the safe word, the way you guys were tickling the bejesus out of me I was lucky I could remember my damned name, let alone a safe word to stop you two from tickling me nearly to death..." Mark said, pointing a finger at Christopher.

"And how were we supposed to have known that?" Christopher asked. "Look, I'm really sorry, if that's what you want to hear, okay? But I really did think that you were playing the scene the whole time. What can I do to make it up to you?"

"Well, I came here to really blast you, *and* I was planning on giving you a taste of your own ticklish medicine as well," Mark said, stepping over to the chair where his suit jacket was, reached into the jacket's pocket and brought out a pair of thick leather wrist restraints with insulated padding on them.

He held them up on a finger, a fiendish look in his dark eyes. Christopher stepped over to Mark, took the restraints from his finger where they dangled and looked them over, his hands trembling, his cock, by now, hard and pounding in his jeans.

"And you were going to lock *me* in these and tickle torture the hell out of me?" Christopher asked.

"Fuck yeah, and seeing as that partner of yours isn't here to protect you and seeing as you're all alone I'm sure we'll have a rip roaring ho, ho, hidey ho time, BUDDY," Mark ranted through clenched teeth as he loomed over the author. "Let's see how loud you can be made to laugh Mr. Tickle Author!"

"Uh Mark, Adam isn't here, but who said I was alone?" Christopher asked with a glint in his eyes.

Suddenly, from behind, the handsome Mark was grabbed by the upper arms by two muscle bound brutes.

"WHA...HEY!" Mark garbled in shock as he was yanked a few inches backward, his arms being twisted behind him at the same time.

"Mark my ticklish, ticklish buddy; may I introduce my two friends, Alex and Dennis?" Christopher asked as Mark struggled to no avail in his captor's vise-like grips. "They happened to be here as consultants for a story I'm working on at the moment. And it looks as if they're about to experience firsthand something just like what I was writing about recently."

While Mark had been ranting on and on at him Christopher had watched as his two buddies emerged silently from the small bedroom where the author had his computer and writing office set up. When Mark had arrived and while he was waiting to gain entrance to Christopher's apartment was when the author had told his buddies that a chicken had just flown into their coop...and to be ready to pounce. While the author and Mark were conversing Christopher prayed that his ticklish buddy would not turn around and see his two muscular brutish buddies making the scene behind the unwitting guy.

"Yeah, real nice to meet you two muscle heads," Mark said through clenched teeth as he continued struggling, his wing-tipped feet slip sliding on the hardwood floor.

"Nice to meet you too Marky boy, the dark haired guy named Alex said as he tightened his grip on Mark's upper arm, right at his bicep curl under his getting wrinkled white shirt. "Christopher told us about you after him and his partner worked you over last time you were here. I've wanted to meet you since hearing about you...BUDDY..."

"Hey Christopher, you want to call off your two brutes here?" Mark called out, watching as Christopher made his way over to the air conditioner in the window and turned it on. "Shit, that contraption wasn't broken after all," Mark seethed.

"Nope, just wanted an excuse to get you loosened up a bit buddy boy," Christopher laughed and held up the leather wrist restraints that Mark had brought with him. "And just what *were* you planning on doing with these my ticklish bud? Tickle the author perhaps? Me thinks not you sexy fuck."

Mark's heart pounded in fear as the wavy haired muscular blond guy named Dennis leaned in real close to his face and kissed him wet and slurpy on the cheek, ala Bugs Bunny. He even licked Mark's face with his very wet tongue.

"SLOB!" Mark ranted at the guy as both men now held him with two hands each at the upper arms. "GAWD, let go of me you guys!"

Christopher stepped back over to his helpless buddy and dangled the wrist restraints in his face.

"You can't imagine how glad, HOW VERY GLAD I am that you decided to stop over here tonight Mark," Christopher said and Mark's jaw dropped a few inches, his face turning almost pale white. "And my two buddies here are equally as glad...if not more-so than I am..."

"Oh no, come on man, Christopher, please, you wouldn't do what I think you're thinking of doing..." Mark pleaded, looked side by side a few times at the two guys holding him tight and hunched his shoulders upwards in a vain attempt to pull free from their grasps. "UUUHHHRRRR..."

As he lifted his shoulders the two muscle brutes held Mark tighter and hoisted him a few inches off the floor, his shoed feet dangling a bit.

"And why not? You're here, my partner is out, chances are your partner is out somewhere on business," Christopher said as Mark dangled off the floor, the two muscular guys lifting him a tad higher yet.

"Damn it Christopher, this one really is a looker," Alex, he with darker hair than Dennis said lustfully.

"And a struggler," Dennis added and chuckled fiendishly.

As he spoke Christopher twisted one of Mark's very erect nipples...

"And if I recall correctly buddy, the last time we got together it was so easy for you because your partner was out of town, is that why you're here now?" Christopher asked and twisted Mark's nipple harder.

"OUCH!" Mark yelled. "Christopher, my partner will get you for this!"

"Ah, but my ticklish buddy, the real question of the moment is, will he get you?" Christopher laughed, squatted down and grabbed Mark's feet by his heels.

He lifted the guy's legs till he was in a prone position, being held aloft now by his upper arms and calves. Christopher lovingly ran his hands under Mark's suit trousers and caressed those nylon sheer socked calves, loving the feel of them against his skin.

"You see, I'm guessing that your partner has no idea where you are at the moment," Christopher laughed and Mark's handsome face took on a look of horror as the author began taking his slip-on shoes off his feet.

"Christopher, NO, NO, don't take my shoes off me man, you don't know what that will do to me..." Mark pleaded miserably and watched then as his shoes left his feet and Christopher dropped them to the floor.

"Ah, but I do know what not having your shoes on your feet will do to you my handsome and ticklish buddy, it will tickle you, that's what it will do..." Christopher laughed and pressed his thumbs against the bottoms of Mark's navy blue nylon socked feet. "It will tickle you bud..."

"OHHHHH, OH NO, NO, HAHAHAHA..." Mark wailed. "Oh

the torture...Christopher, you know how the slightest touch makes me crazy! You know how hyper tickle sensitive I am...OH PLEASE..."

"Yes, I know Mark, I know, which is why I and my buddies here intend to take full advantage of that," Christopher replied, kissed Mark's socked feet a few times, inhaled their sexy musty leathery and silk odor and then lowered them to the floor.

"Lock him in these guys," Christopher said, handing the leather restraints to Alex.

"NO, NO, Christopher, this is unacceptable man!" Mark ranted as the two muscle brutes forced his shirt down his arms and off him, leaving him bare chested now in all his musculature and glory.

While they had let go of him he tried to make a break for it and head for the door to the author's apartment. He didn't care if he left shirtless, he just did not feel like being tickle tortured to the point of insanity all over again in this place. But Alex and Dennis were not only hugely muscular, they were very fast. Alex grabbed the ticklish guy by one arm as Christopher grabbed him by the other, stopping him in his sheer socked tracks.

"Fuckers, fucking fucks, just like last time!" Mark prattled as Alex and Christopher held his arms behind him and Dennis did the honors of locking his wrists in the leather restraints he had brought with him. "OH FUCKING FUCKS!"

The sound of the restraints locking around the ticklish guy's wrists was music to the author's ears, however, it spelled doom to Mark himself.

"So tell me my ticklish buddy, do you know the safe word this time out?" Christopher teased his captured prize and as Mark stood rigid and terrified the author stole a few sucks on one of his nipples.

"Bastard," Mark gasped as his nipple was sucked on.

"Nope, that is most definitely not the safe word," Christopher laughed and placed a hand on Mark's belt buckle.

A few moments later Mark was standing between Christopher's muscular brutish buddies. His wrists had been locked in the leather restraints that he had brought with him and his nipples were bubbled up to the sizes of new pencil erasers, seeing as not just Christopher but Alex and Dennis as well had made sport of sucking and twisting them.

"Oh the irony," Mark cried as the guy named Alex reinforced the restraints on his wrists as Dennis held him tightly in place so Christopher could slide his suit pants down his legs.

"You're a regular poet," Alex teased the captured tickle slave and again sloppily kissed his cheek.

This time Mark realized he was in no position to call the guy a slob, or anything else for that matter... When his suit pants were pooled around his socked ankles the handsome Mark stepped out of them and stood there now in just his sheer navy blue socks and white cotton briefs by Calvin Klein. He watched miserably and with a feeling of total humiliation as his suit pants were added to the pile of his clothing on the nearby chair.

"You fuckers, you guys will pay for this," Mark seethed.

"Pay for it?" Alex laughed and squeezed one of Mark's ass cheeks through his briefs. "You ticklish guy, we're getting it for free, we aren't paying for shit!"

Alex and Dennis stood at Mark's sides, stealing squeezes on his hard and delectable ass cheeks as they looked like two coconuts in his white briefs. Mark's cock was fear hard and tenting his briefs in front as Christopher turned to him now.

"Christopher, release me now," Mark demanded as he struggled in the wrist restraints.

"What? And have you miss out on the new device I bought recently?" Christopher asked his captive, sounding totally fiendish.

Mark's jaw dropped when he saw Christopher look toward the closed bedroom doors, the room where he had spent his last visit, being tickle tortured for what seemed like hours on end.

"Knowing you I can just imagine what sort of device you have in there," Mark seethed.

"Yes, and how fortunate that you should have stopped by tonight," Christopher teased and twisted one of Mark's nipples again.

"Fucking fuck man, what is it with you and my nips? I told you to leave my damned nipples alone," Mark prattled, still struggling in the wrist restraints to no avail.

"Mark, Mark, you are in no position to be telling me anything," Christopher said and then in a blinding motion trailed his fingertips over and over Mark's sexy sides and his ribs.

"YAHHHHHHHH!" Mark suddenly cackled.

"See? I told you guys he's extremely ticklish," Christopher said.

"NO, NO, CHRISTOPHER, oh GOD, don't do this to me again man," Mark pleaded as three sets of hands were then tickling his ribs and sides. "AAAAAHHHHH! HA, HA, HA, HA, HA, HA, HA!"

"Let's make him dance guys," Christopher said fiendishly.

Mark found himself dancing between the three men, slipping and sliding in his sheer socks on the slippery hardwood floor. He involuntarily twirled and turned in his vain attempts to escape the tickling onslaught.

"HAHAHAHAHAHAHA! AHHHHH you fucking fucked up fuckers!" Mark screeched.

"What's the safe word buddy?" Christopher asked, gripping Marks' upper arm tight and wedged a fingertip in his underarm pit, twirling it as he went.

"OOOOOOOOO! HAHAHAHAHAHAHA!" was the poor guy's response.

"Nope, that is definitely not the safe word either bud," Christopher laughed and resumed tickling Mark's ribs and sides along with his two buddies. "Come on Mark, make like John Travolta and dance the night away...oh you sexy ticklish guy...HA!"

It seemed that whichever way the captured guy turned and danced he was treated to an onslaught of finger tickling... At one point Dennis held the guy still by his upper arms while Christopher and Alex tickled his stomach area. Mark really screamed his laughter when the guys took turns poking their fingertips deeply into his belly button...

"I thought you said we were going to tickle him in that device you have in the bedroom," Alex said as he scribbled his fingers over Mark's abdomen.

"We will, this is just warming him up," Christopher said and when Dennis let go of the tickle captive's arms Mark found himself again twirling and dancing for the three guys as they tickled, tickled, tickled and tickled him some more.

"YAAAAHHHHHH! HAHAHAHAHAHA!" Mark screeched, lifting his socked feet up high as he danced and twirled in ticklish agony. "PLEASE, PLEASE, stop this! Come on you guys, you've had your fun with me here!" When Dennis reached down and squeezed one of Mark's inner thighs the handsome stripped executive nearly jumped out of his sheer socks.

"AAAAARRRRRHHH, no, no, not my thighs!" Mark reeled. "HAHAHAHAHAHA!"

The three guys squatted down at Mark's thighs, hunkered around him and took turns squeezing the bejesus out of his thigh skin, twisting it, tickling him into a new frenzy...

"AAAAAAAYYYYY you bastards," Mark laughed. "I'm having trouble balancing myself here..."

Then, in a sweeping motion Mark found himself being lifted from the floor and the next thing he knew the muscle brute named Alex had him slung over one of his huge broad shoulders. Mark was breathless, sweating and gasping...

"Christopher, let me go, oh GOD, let me go," Mark pleaded as he was carried toward the bedroom, Christopher leading the way.

As the three men entered the bedroom with their tickle prize Alex tossed Mark bodily upwards.

"AAAAAWWWWWWW!" Mark roared, looking at the ceiling as he flew up, thinking he would hit the floor and break his back for sure, but rather Alex caught the guy in his huge arms, holding him now in a position of a groom lifting his bride and carrying her over the threshold. "OOOFFFFFF!"

"Gotcha you handsome guy," Alex laughed and kissed Mark on the cheek.

"Son of a bitch," Mark said, tucking his socked feet under him as he was carried into the bedroom.

When Mark saw the device at the foot of the queen sized bed he not only moved his socked feet further under himself he also curled his toes back. The poor guy gulped hard in terror at the sight of the...

"Stocks, wooden stocks..." Mark said miserably as Alex lowered him onto the bed and Dennis and Christopher did the honors of securing the guy's navy blue sheer socked feet into the wooden structure.

"OH GOD Christopher, is this the device you said you bought?" Mark asked, watching miserably as his sexy socked feet were locked tightly into the stocks' holes.

"This and some other implements bud," Christopher said jovially, leaned down and kissed Mark's socked toes a few times, holding his now imprisoned feet by his arches.

"Spread eagle him guys," Christopher said and then opened a dresser drawer.

A few moments later Mark was laying on the bed with his arms spread wide and his wrists locked in leather restraints attached to the edges of the headboard. His navy blue sheer socked feet looked totally sexy and helpless in the stocks as he wiggled them a bit... The way he was tethered to the bed, stretched out, did not allow the guy much wiggle room whatsoever.

"GAWD, I'm stretched tighter than a new drum here! Christopher, please, PLEASE, let me go man," Mark pleaded. "I did not come here for this, this time..."

"No? Where do you usually go?" Christopher asked as he opened a medium-sized box.

Alex and Dennis were hunkered down at Mark's sides, each of them slurping, sucking and nursing on one of his over-sized nipples each. They twirled their tongues over the very tips of Mark's jutted up nubs and then meanly slurped his tits greedily back into their mouths, getting a few good gasps and grunts out of the tied guy. Mark's cock was hard and dripping pre seed in his white briefs. His kiwi-sized balls were outlined in the thin white material.

"FUCKERS, Christopher, get these goons of yours off my goddamned tits," Mark seethed and raised his head off the bed, looking angrily up at his captor. "You can't do this to me again! Last time was bad enough..."

"HA, you think that the last time Adam and I had you here was bad my ticklish buddy," Christopher laughed. "By the time we're done tickling and roasting you here today you'll be begging me and my muscle buddies to get you off...and I know that having your tits sucked does get you off...eventually... but first we'll need to really tickle you...just to get you into the right frame of mind..."

With a smirk Christopher looked over at the clock on his night-table.

"I think we'll go for better then three hours this time, what do you think Mark?" Christopher said fiendishly. "How does that make you feel?"

"OH GAWD..." Mark bantered miserably.

Christopher opened the medium sized box and held up a set of prickly looking shaving brushes...all of them in various sizes and shapes...

"OH GOD, no, not that Christopher," Mark gasped.

Alex and Dennis stopped sucking the trapped guy's nipples and stepped to Christopher's sides. Tears were in Mark's eyes as he watched each of the guys help themselves to one of the prickly shaving brushes each...

Alex positioned himself by Mark's neck and face...

Dennis positioned himself at Mark's mid-section and armpits...

And Christopher of course hunkered down at his tickle captive's trapped socked feet in the stocks...

Mark's eyes darted back and forth at all the guys as they took up position around him. The ticklish guy felt like a sacrificial lamb on an altar at that moment...

"G-guys, pl-please, don't, don't tickle me..." Mark pleaded, watching as Christopher pressed his nose against one of his feet in the stocks.

Mark wiggled his toes involuntarily and Christopher kissed them...

"Okay Mark, before we begin would you care for a blindfold?" Christopher teased.

"Fuck, fuck, fuck," Mark seethed and yanked fruitlessly on the bindings on his wrists.

Then, a micro second later Mark was howling and laughing his head off as the three guys tickled his most sensitive areas with the shaving brushes...

Alex ran his soft horse haired round brush over Mark's neck, under his ears and all over his face.

Dennis trailed his long sleek prickly brush bristles down Mark's chest, twirled it against his stomach region and glided it along his sides and ribs. He trailed the brush back up and paid special attention to Mark's erect nipples, affording them equal tickle torture time...

Mark laughed and squealed, spittle flew from the sides of his mouth and at times he whooped and ranted...

Christopher was hunkered down at Mark's glorious navy blue sheer socked feet. As he trailed his thin shaving brush up and down the bottoms of the guy's tootsies Mark's feet flicked and twitched involuntarily in the stocks. Christopher looked at those feet as if they were the ninth and tenth wonders of the world and he inhaled their sweaty, leathery and silky aroma; all the while tickle torturing the bejesus out of them.

"STOP, STOP, STOPPPPP THIS, oh MY GAWD YOU GUYS, please, PLEASE STOP THIS!" Mark keened, his head lifted up off the bed as Alex tickle tortured the back of his neck now. "HAHAHAHAHAHAHA! CHRISTOPHER please!"

"Just wait till we roll your underpants down in front and tickle your cock and balls my ticklish bud," Mark heard Christopher say and he laughed even harder.

"OH NO, you, you wouldn't!" Mark sputtered.

"You should know from the last time that I would buddy," Christopher said and glided his brush over the tips of Mark's socked toes. "Like those stocks I have your feet in?"

"HAHAHAHAHAHAHAHAHAHAHA!" was Mark's response.

"Good, because I plan to keep these sexy feeties of yours in them for most of the time we have you here..." Christopher said.

"Looks like you got yourself a whole new story to write based on this huh Christopher?" Dennis asked as he tickle tortured Mark's stomach, twirling his bristles of the brush over and over his smooth skin.

"Sure as hell looks like it Dennis," Christopher replied and then using a brush on the bottom of one of Mark's feet, Christopher trailed his fingernails of his other hand over the bottom of Mark's other foot.

"WHOOOOOOOOO!" was the familiar sound that emanated from the tied up and stocked guy, a sound that Christopher remembered from the last time he and his partner had tickle tortured him.

"WAHHHHHHHHAHAHAHAHAHAHA!"

Mark's peals of laughter suddenly reached a higher crescendo when Dennis started tickling one of his very exposed armpits with his shaving brush and tickling the guy's other armpit with his fingertips.

"NO, NOOOOOO, OOOOOOOO NO, not my damned pits you bastard!" Mark reeled and squirmed as much as his bindings would allow, which was not much. "HA, HA, HA, HA, HA, HA, HA, HA, HA, HA, HA!"

Again the tickled guy lifted his head and looked down at Christopher as the author was doing the honors of now lick-tickling the bottoms of his sheer socked feet.

"CHRISTOPHER, this fucking guy is tickling my damned pits!" Mark screeched and Alex gently pushed his head back down on the bed, and resumed trailing his wavy haired shaving brush over and over the guy's neck and under his ears.

"Yes, and isn't it just too funny Mark?" Christopher chided his ticklish buddy.

Dennis dug in deep with his fingertips and shaving brush in Mark's armpits, sending the guy into breathless gasps, grunts and shockwaves of laughter...

Christopher was again trailing his shaving brush over and up and down the bottoms of Mark's sheer socked feet, over his toes, deep in his arches and over the tops of them as well. Christopher marveled at the way Mark's feet twitched and danced in the stocks. The author could not resist kissing those feet every few moments as they sweated and were more and more scented in the socks with each passing ticklish moment...

"CHRISTOPHER, oh GOD please, PLEASE stop, even for a minute or two, HAHAHAHAHA, I-I'm laughing myself to death here! EEEEEEEEE!"

"Double time guys," Christopher said and gestured toward the box of shaving brushes.

A few moments later, to Mark's horror, all three of his tickle captors had two brushes each in hand...

Alex was using his two brushes on Mark's face, his under-neck, under his ears and against his Adam's apple... All Mark could do was keep his head pressed to the bed as the guy tickle tortured his head, neck and ears areas...

Dennis trailed two prickly brushes around and around and around Mark's sweaty stomach region, over his nipples at the same time, deep in his armpits and down the undersides of his stretched out muscular arms...

Christopher used two brushes to tickle torture the bottoms and arches of Mark's socked feet locked in the stocks...

The three guys moved their brushes all over the ticklish guy at what felt to him to be at least sixty to a hundred miles per hour...

"YAAAAAAHHHHHH HAHAHAHAHAHAHAHA!" Mark screeched crazily. "F-F-FUCKERS!"

After a good (bad?) forty-five minutes of tickle torture the three guys stopped tickling Mark with their shaving brushes. The poor guy was breathless, gasping, choking and sweating profusely as he lay there helpless. A few last peals of laughter escaped him as he watched the guys place their brushes back in the box. His underpants and socks were drenched in sweat and stinking in a manly way.

"OOOOOOOOO, th-thank you, thank you guys," Mark stammered laughingly. "Thank you for stopping...OOOOOOOOO..."

He arched his sweaty head back and stretched his muscular torso as much as the bindings would allow.

"Looks like he could use a cool drink Christopher," Dennis said, looking down at the bound up and stocked guy.

"I'll get him some water," Christopher said and left the bedroom.

Mark looked up at Alex and Dennis and quipped miserably, "I hope you muscle heads are having a good time here...at my damned expense..."

The two muscle brutes hunkered down at Mark's socked feet in the stocks and stole a few licks and slurps on them, really sucking the sweaty juice from his toes...

"Fuckers, bastards, capturing me was a shitty thing to do..." Mark murmured as his cock pounded in his sweat sopped briefs while the two guys played suck and slurp with his sheer socked feet. "I was telling the truth earlier, what Christopher and his partner did to me last time was downright mean..."

But it seemed to the bound up ticklish guy that the two muscle head's were either ignoring his rant, or they were just too transfixed with the taste of his socked feet to care...

A short while later Christopher was feeding Mark a glass of cold water through a straw. The author held his tied up buddies' head up by the back of the neck as he sipped the water down.

"Feeling okay?" Christopher asked when Mark was done drinking.

"Yeah, yeah, just great," Mark responded as he lowered his head back down to the bed. "Just the way I figured on spending this evening..."

"Glad to hear that bud, because now we will resume tickling you," Christopher chuckled as he set the empty water glass down on his night table.

"OH NO, NO, please, NO!" Mark pleaded, watching miserably as Christopher rolled his briefs down in front and tucked the sweaty thin material under his succulent looking balls.

Alex, Dennis and Christopher all looked hungrily at the tickle captive's cock as it stuck straight up, big and beefy and throbbing, the green veins in it paramount, and pre cum oozing from his wide sexy slit... Mark watched helplessly as the three guys stole sniffs and whiffs of his manhood and sweaty scrotum.

"Jeez, I just want to scoff it down," Dennis said softly.

"First we tickle it, and his balls," Christopher said as he again picked up the box of shaving brushes.

"OHHHHHH, you bastards, not my damned family jewels," Mark pleaded as each of his captors helped themselves to two brushes each.

A few scant seconds later Mark was again singing his laughter in high C's as the three guys made sport of tickling his most private of regions.

"YAHHHHHHHHHH! HAW, HAW, HAW, HAW, HAW, HAW, HAW!" Mark crowed wildly, bucking, thrashing and writhing atop the bed as much as his bindings would again allow.

With his head raised and a maniacal looking smile on his face the poor guy laughed and cawed as he watched his captors tickling his manhood...with the shaving brushes.

Alex used two wavy brushes to tickle under and over and around Mark's sweaty balls, really sending churns and ticklish chills up the bound guy's spine...

Dennis used two thin haired brushes to tease Mark's pre cum oozing slit, twirling the brush tips bristles in his piss hole, really getting the guy to sing his laughter...

Christopher swirled two brushes over and over the shaft of Mark's erect cock, teasing him, tormenting the very fuck out of him...

"OHHHHHH you bastards, when I'm out of this you'll pay for this! HAHAHAHA!" Mark cackled loudly in between powerful bouts of laughter.

"It will be quite a while before you're out of this my ticklish buddy,"

Christopher said meanly and pressed his brushes harder against Mark's throbbing shaft.

"GAWD, tickling my cock is making me want to shoot a load," Mark roared. "HAW, HAW, HAW, HAW, HAW, HAW, HEEEEEEEEEEEE!"

"You mean to say that you haven't wanted to shoot a load since you got here bud?" Christopher teased the trapped guy.

"HAHAHAHAHAHAHAHAHA!" Mark laughed uncontrollably.

The three guy's tickling Mark all laughed as well, they did not laugh with him however, rather they laughed at him and the predicament he had so unwittingly thrust himself into...

"OH GAWD, when will this stop? When will you let me go? When will you stop ticking me? HAHAHAHAHAHAHAHAHAHAHAHAHAHA!" Mark reeled.

When the three men stopped tickling his cock and balls Mark's erection was like a thing alive as it twitched, flicked and swung back and forth between his legs. His balls were churning, no doubt cooking his cum and oodles and oodles of droplets of pre cum oozed from the guy's wide sexy piss hole. Mark was breathless as he watched the three guys now tonguing his manhood. Christopher was busy slurping at the crown of Mark's towering erection, really sending chills of frustration through the hyper ticklish and most definitely over-sensitized at that point guy. Alex was busying himself licking and slurping at Mark's shaft while Dennis alternated between licking his balls and also licking at the other side of his throbbing shaft. The three tongues, sets of lips and mouths all over his cock and balls were sending the bound up guy into orbit. Needless to say his head was spinning...

"OHHHHHHHHH, fuckers, that, that feels awesome, better than being tickled into insanity," Mark panted, sweat pouring off him everywhere at that point.

He wiggled his trapped socked feet in the stocks as the three guys continued worshipping his manhood.

"FUCKING fuck, I'm getting close Christopher," Mark whispered, his head raised, watching as the man who had manufactured his capture seemed to be in ecstasy as he ate the droplets of pre seed off his cock-tip.

Alex and Dennis lovingly sucked and slurped and licked at Mark's shaft and balls...

When they each sucked one his balls into their mouths and slurped hard while Christopher sucked his crown at the same time Mark thought how if he weren't tied and stocked to the bed that he would have flown off it...

"OHHHHHHH! ARRRHHHHHHHH!" Mark was grunting and groaning a few minutes later as he shot a whopper of a load, right down Christopher's throat as the author greedily sucked and slurped and nursed at his cock. "FUCKING GUYS!"

Mark stretched himself tighter on the bed and his socked feet twitched in the stocks...

As Christopher siphoned Mark's load from his cock Alex and Dennis sucked heartily at his balls as they spewed forth what was in them...

"OOOOOOOOOOO..." Mark swooned a few seconds later when he was done spurting his mess.

Christopher licked his lips and looked down at his tickle buddy in an almost loving manner...

"Can't thank you enough for stopping by here tonight Mark," Christopher teased.

"So glad I could make your night," Mark replied sarcastically. "Now how about letting me go at this point huh? If you recall, last time, after I shot my load you and Adam did let me go..."

Christopher smiled fiendishly and he and his two buddies looked at each other...

"You know guys, it's pretty well known when it comes to this tickle kink that after a guy shoots his load he becomes nearly ten times more tickle sensitive," Christopher said, sounding comical.

"OH NO, NO, Christopher please, don't do this!" Mark begged, thrashing again in his wrist bindings, his socked feet dancing stupidly in the stocks.

Mark pursed his lips together, a look of defeat coming over his handsome and sweaty face and he murmured the words, "oh shit" when he saw the three men looking at him hungrily...

The ticklish guy wondered how much more he would be able to endure...

He watched then as Christopher left the bedroom, leaving him again in the care of Alex and Dennis...

"Do you suppose that's true, what Christopher just said?" Alex asked Dennis as the two men stood at the foot of the bed, right over Mark's stocked and trapped feet.

"You mean about a guy being even more tickle sensitive after he cums?" Dennis replied, sounding humorous.

As the two men spoke they were gently massaging the palms of their hands over and over the bottoms of Mark's soft socked feet...

"I suppose there's only one sure way to find out," Dennis laughed and then he and Alex were scribbling their fingertips all over and up and down the bottoms of Mark's socked feet.

"OHHHHHH NO, NO, YOU sons of bitches," Mark screamed at the sudden tickle onslaught.

"Yep, it does ring true, he's laughing louder and harder than he did before he shot his load," Alex quipped and pressed the tips of his fingers harder against the bottom of Mark's socked foot that he was tickling.

Mark felt totally helpless as he lay there laughing his head off and being tickled, tickled, tickled... As he laughed his head off, watching as Christopher Trevor's muscle buddies tickled his feet in the stocks his semi hard cock twitched between his legs...

A short while later Mark found himself off the bed and standing on his socked feet. The handsome captured tickle prize was clad now in just his OTC navy blue sheer socks, his briefs having been unceremoniously removed when the two muscle brutes had temporarily un-tethered him and hauled him off the bed. His socked feet had been freed from the stocks as well, but for the moment the handsome high-socked executive knew he was going nowhere. Feeling frustrated and beyond riled at that point Mark stood with his wrists locked behind him in the leather restraints that he himself had brought and his white cloth handkerchief had been tied over his eyes now as his blindfold... As his two muscle buddies set up the "equipment" for the next tickle session Christopher held Mark by his upper arm as the guy leaned against a wall. Christopher held a bottle of mineral water to Mark's quivering lips that the guy sipped through a straw.

"Feeling good buddy?" Christopher asked his blindfolded tickle captive.

"Yeah, feeling real good, more like feeling totally used and abused," Mark seethed behind his blindfold. "Bastard you can be Christopher, what's the point of all this?"

"Just having fun with you buddy, just having some real good old fashioned tickle fun with you," the author replied and fed Mark some more water.

"We're just about ready here Christopher," Mark heard Alex say.

While he had been standing there restrained and blindfolded Mark was able to hear some sort of furniture being moved around the bedroom...

"Jeez..." Mark bantered and his cock stiffened at the impending tickling he knew he was to endure yet again.

"So, tell me my handsome buddy, do you feel that you've gotten the revenge you came here for?" Christopher asked Mark, squeezing his arm tighter.

"Fucker," the high socked executive replied through clenched teeth...

"Okay Christopher, bring him on over," Alex said then and Mark felt himself being guided forward by his arms.

"What now guys? What the fuck now?" Mark quibbled miserably.

When the blindfold was whipped off him and he saw the set-up Mark's jaw dropped and he said, "Oh fuck me, this is just like last time when you had me here Christopher..."

The two muscle brutes tended to setting the ticklish guy up...

Mark found himself kneeling on a chair, facing forward, his chest pressed against the back of the chair. Alex and Dennis tied him tight to the chair-back at his upper torso as Christopher did the honors of binding his socked feet tightly together. On a table set up in front of the chair he was kneeling on Mark saw an array of high-powered electric toothbrushes...

"Bastards should have kept me blindfolded..." Mark said despondently.

Soon, all three of the guys, armed with the electric toothbrushes turned up to their highest power, were tickling Mark at all his sensitive spots. His hard cock was thrust between the chair's rungs he was leaning against and his balls were tied off just so. Mark's cock was as trapped as the rest of him was...

"YAAAAAARRRRHHHHHH! HAHAHAHAHAHA!" Mark screeched in a high pitched crescendo as the electric toothbrushes were glided over him.

Alex was having a ball teasing Mark's jutted up nipples with his toothbrush, tickling them till the guy felt that his nipples were being cooked. Mark watched with his head lowered and laughing wildly as Alex trailed his toothbrush down his torso to his stomach region...

"You suck man, YOU REALLY SUCK, HAHAHAHAHAHAHA!"

Mark cried out laughingly.

Alex grinned at the poor guy and tickled his belly button real deep with his electric toothbrush.

From behind him Mark was being tickled by Dennis and Christopher...

Dennis was trailing his electric toothbrush up and down Mark's muscular back while Christopher was tickling his socked feet with his...

The ropes held the thrashing tickle victim real tight and fast as he knelt perched on the chair and being made to laugh uncontrollably...

A while later Mark was blindfolded yet again and as he was tickled the guys took turns sucking his hard cock. He was made to guess who was sucking his cock. If he guessed wrong an additional ten minutes of tickle time was added onto his torture. If he guessed correctly only an additional five minutes of tickle time was added...

"Sadistic little game," Mark intoned as his cock was sucked. "Somehow I think that's Alex sucking my pud now..."

"KEEE-rect my ticklish buddy," Mark heard Christopher chuckle. "Now we tickle you for five minutes..."

Once more the electric toothbrushes were used to tickle Mark...

"AAAYYYYYYY! HAHAHAHAHAHA!" Mark laughed crazily.

The game went on and on until Christopher once again made the ticklish guy shoot his load and scoffed it down...

"Fucking guys, when is this going to stop?" Mark asked breathlessly as his cock was held captive in Christopher's mouth and he seemed to cum and cum endlessly.

Mark felt hands caressing him and he swooned then as Alex and Dennis slurped his nipples a few times, as Christopher drank down the rest of his seed...

"Fuck yeah..." Mark whispered.

Three and a half hours later Mark freshly showered and dressed in his business attire emerged from Christopher's bathroom...

"Are you okay?" Christopher asked, sitting on the couch and taking in the gloriously handsome sight before him.

"Yeah, as okay as I'm going to be I suppose," Mark said, straightening his tie as he stood before his author buddy. "Where are Alex and Dennis?"

"They had another appointment to get to," Christopher said, getting to his feet and pulling Mark into his arms, hugging him tight.

"Hmm, another tickle victim waiting to be captured eh?" Mark asked as Christopher kissed the side of his neck and Mark hugged him back.

"You might say that," Christopher said and finished straightening Mark's tie for him. "So, was this to your satisfaction? Did we make your fantasy a reality as much as we did last time?"

Mark smiled a devilish smile and said, "That and then some, having Alex and Dennis participate this time really made it horrendous."

"And you played your part just as well too," Christopher said, walking Mark toward the door of the apartment.

"Thanks, but I really should be on my way now," Mark said. "I really appreciate this again Christopher. You're the best when it comes to tickle fantasies..."

"So are you Mark," Christopher said and when Mark opened the door and was about to step out of the apartment he saw Alex and Dennis blocking his way.

"Thought we would give you a bit of a bonus before you headed on home Marky boy," Christopher laughed.

"OH NO, no," Mark reeled as Alex and Dennis hoisted him from under his arms and carried him back into the apartment.

As the door slammed shut Mark shouted, "Christopher this was not part of the plan!" and his shoes fell from his feet...

# ABOUT THE EDITOR

## Christopher Trevor

Christopher Trevor was born in July 1963 and grew up in New York City. As soon as he was old enough to know how he began writing fiction and has been writing gay erotic/fetish stories for the past ten to twelve years at this point. He became an avid reader as well from the time he knew how and reads everything from fiction, to non-fiction to biographies of interesting and unusual people, people who have made a difference or who have paved the way for others. Christopher attributes his writing artistic inspiration to artists such as Etienne, Tom of Finland, Tagame, The Hun, and most notably Joe T, who Christopher has  had the pleasure of speaking with and even meeting over the last few years.

Christopher states, "Joe T encouraged me to write about my fetish because I was embarrassed about it at the time. Joe T said that when we are embarrassed about something that makes it even more enticing somehow." Christopher totally agreed and never stopped writing in this genre. Erotic writers who inspired Christopher Trevor were: Tom Shaw (author of "That Day at the Quarry), C.S. White (author of Big Sur), Larry Townsend (author of countless erotic novels), and Mason Powell (author of the classic story "The Brig.")

Christopher discovered that not only did he enjoy writing erotic tales but that after his first bondage experience he had a genuine flair for it. Writing to erotic oriented magazines about his first bondage experience truly opened the floodgates for Christopher where this style of writing is concerned. Christopher thanks the handsome and muscular "Greg" for that experience way back in time. Christopher took "Creative Writing" courses every semester during his high school years and while other friends of his stopped writing what they loved to write about as time went on Christopher never let a day go by when he didn't write something... "I feel that if I don't write every day I will die," Christopher has said many times over.

Foot fetish stories and all things related; spanking fetish, erotic shaving, muscle bondage, tickle torture, and hardcore stories are just a few of the areas of gay eroticism that Christopher enjoys writing about and inspiring in others as well. As one internet buddy said to Christopher where the black socks fetish is concerned, "Until I started talking with you I never gave a thought to my socks when I got dressed for work in the morning. Now when I pull my dress socks on every morning I get a chill up my spine."

Christopher is proud of the erotic effect he has on people...

Christopher Trevor is also the author of:

**The Executive Guide to Foot Fetishism and Office Discipline**

1-887895-36-1

**Executive Ties That Bind**
1-887895-37-X

**Don't! Stop! That Tickles!**
1-887895-31-0

**The Taming of Dominick**
1-887895-45-0

**Timmy and The Hong Kong Tailor**
1-887895-30-2

**Love, Torture and Redemption**
1-887895-32-9

**Timmys Ticklish Trials**
978-1-887895-74-3

**The Gym Instructor**
978-1-887895-44-6

**Milked**
978-1-887895-66-8

**Erotic Street Blues**
978-1-887895-97-2

**The Abusive Wager**
978-1-887895-04-0

**Terry's Appointment and Other Tickling Stories**
978-1-934625-08-8

**The Military File**
978-1-934625-21-7

**Quirks**
978-1-934625-24-8

**Timmy and the Evil Dr. Vonvellicator**
978-1-934625-42-2

**Blackmail**
978-1-934625-47-7

Look for them where you bought this book or TheNazcaPlainsCorp.com

www.ingramcontent.com/pod-product-compliance
Lightning Source LLC
Chambersburg PA
CBHW071225260626
47162CB00004B/1428